Copyright Page

The Way Love Goes

Printed in the United States of America

First Printing, 2020

ISBN: 1660034246

ISBN-13: 9781660034246

DISCLAIMER

This is a work of fiction. Names, characters, businesses, places, events and incidents are either the products of the author's imagination or used in a fictitious manner. Any resemblance to actual persons, living or dead, or actual events is purely coincidental.

ACKNOWLEDGEMENT

It's a must that I acknowledge all who read, review and recommend my books to others. I appreciate the love.

I'd also like to acknowledge my true blue, Sweet. Shon was exactly what the protagonist needed on the pages, and you are just as dope off the pages. I appreciate your patience and trusting that I was going to get to "us" ☺. Love you!

If you haven't already, please check out books 1, 2 and 3 from the Love Collection

The Way Love Goes

By Vy Antenette

Chapter One

Whitney drove with the windows up and the music on as she listened to Jon B and Tupac lyrically question if some woman was "still down." Her vibrating cell phone stole her attention, as she glanced at the screen to see who was calling, hoping it wasn't her father again. Lately, he had been alluding to something, but not revealing what it was, and it was beginning to annoy her. One look at the caller ID, and she knew exactly what the call was about. Whitney peeked at the clock on her dashboard and quickly calculated whether she could make a stop and still get to her appointment with Dr. Blakemore on time. The fact that she was stressed and needing a quick release altered her judgment, causing her to accept the call. The voice on the other end confirmed her assumption. She gave an estimated time of arrival before making a sharp U-turn, heading toward one of her most trusted sponsors.

Whitney arrived just as Patrick's parents were pulling out of the driveway with camping gear strapped to the top of the car. She waited down the road until their car was no longer in sight and then carefully drove her black BMW inside the garage. When the doors closed behind her, she got out, opened her trunk, and retrieved her teal duffle bag.

"God, I missed you!" Patrick's ocean blue eyes confirmed his words.

"Then why aren't you down on your knees, panting," she scoffed.

"I'm sorry, Mistress Xxxtasy." Patrick immediately dropped on all fours and looked at the floor, his blonde locks falling neatly in place.

Whitney used her high heels to nudge his forehead and raise his head. He kept his eyes downward. "Look at me," she commanded.

When they made eye contact, she asked, "What did you just call me?"

"I meant Maitresse. Please forgive me, Maitresse Xxxtasy," he begged.

Whitney reached into her bag, pulled out a spiked collar, and placed it around his neck. Once she attached the leash, she led him into the house, up the stairs, and into his bedroom.

"Stand up and bend over the edge of the bed. I see someone has forgotten their manners," she scolded. "That's going to cost you!"

Whitney waited until her subject did as told. His semi-erect penis caused her to smirk. She removed the paddle from the duffle and patted her open palm.

"I am a lady, sub. I'm your lady. I'm also your master, who prefers to be called Maitresse, not Mistress. You know this, Patrick. Yet, you defy my wishes."

"Please forgive me, Maitresse. It's been so long since I've seen you that I for—" *Whack!*

Before he could finish his sentence, Whitney had spanked him with the paddle and was immediately disappointed by his lackluster response. She examined his attire and concluded the thin material was too much clothing. "Take it off," she commanded.

The sound of creaking steps caused them both to remain silent.

"Pat, you still here," a male's voice called.

"Shit that's my dad," Patrick whispered. "He can't see me like this?"

"Stay here, I'll let him know you're in the bathroom or something." Whitney went into the hallway and closed the door behind her, as Patrick's father approached. "Oh hey, Jack, Patrick is um, he's in the bathroom."

His father looked down at her feet and then met her eyes where lust began to show in his.

"This is not the time," she grunted.

"Well when is? I need you so badly." Jack began to pant like an overheated dog and walk towards her.

Whitney placed her hands on his chest and tried turning her face away from his prying mouth. Her hardened nipples caught his attention and he placed his mouth on her left breast. She slapped him.

"Keep it up and I'll scream!"

He became nervous. "Okay, alright. Just be available when I get back from my trip." He walked into his room briefly and back toward the stairs, but not before patting her behind.

When Whitney returned to the room, Patrick was fully naked, causing her to smile. She spanked him once, and then again, and again, and several more times, until his member was fully stiffened and his ass was the color of candied apples. She turned him around and pushed down on his shoulders until he was on his knees and his face was a tongue's length away from her lady parts.

"Lick the kitty, Patrick!" She pulled his head into her groin and watched as he did his best to please her. Even though oral sex wasn't Patrick's strong point, she made him do it simply for the power and control it provided her.

Once she was fed up with the subpar activity, she pushed him away and made him stand. She then gave him fellatio and played with his sack until she felt his body jerk.

She reached up and smacked him across the face. "Did I tell you it was okay to cum?"

"No, no, Maitresse, you did not."

Whitney stood and kissed Patrick on his mouth. If nothing else, she couldn't deny that he was one of the best kissers she'd ever had and she hated that she'd waited so long to experience it.

"Do you want to cum?" she asked politely.

He nodded incessantly.

Whitney ordered him to get a condom and watched as he walked the short distance to his closet, open a shoe box, and pull out a foil wrapper. While Patrick put on the condom, Whitney massaged her clitoris. The sensation was much more satisfying than what Patrick had given her just moments ago.

When she saw that he had completed the task, she told him to lie down. Whitney climbed on top of him and rode him reverse cowgirl style. Patrick held onto her hips and grunted every time she grinded on his member. The louder his grunts, the stiffer he became. That was her indication that he was ready to release. She yanked on his balls and massaged them until Patrick called out in ecstasy. In less than ten minutes, she had completed her mission and was waiting to be paid.

"You know, I really wish you'd consider being mine full time. I'll eventually be making a lot of money, and can buy you whatever you want. You know that, right?" Patrick asked her.

"It's not about the money," she reminded him. Whitney walked into his private bathroom and cleaned herself up. "It's about the freedom to do whatever I want, to whomever I want, whenever I want to."

"I told you, I'm in love with you. We've been seeing each other for over six years, and I'm kinda outgrowing this lifestyle. I want us to be a *normal* couple," he confessed.

Patrick was one of the only boys who truly liked and accepted Whitney for who she was, not what she could offer. They had become close in tenth grade, but he didn't officially become a sponsor until their prom night, when he'd begged her to do to him what he had heard she'd done to some of the other boys at their school.

"Listen, Whitney, I love you and I have for a really long time. I tried letting you know I want to spend the rest of my life with you in so many ways, but it's like you don't even care."

Whitney sighed. "It's not that I don't care, Patrick. It's just that I'm not ready. For crying out loud, I don't even know what love is. So how can I give you what I haven't given myself?" Whitney was exasperated and tired of talking about it. That was why she'd distanced herself from him. Had she not been horny and missing him a little, she would've ignored his call as well.

"Look, I don't want to upset you. Just don't give up on us, okay?"

Whitney ignored his statement, kissed him, and packed up her things. When he handed her the envelope with her money in it, she kissed him on the lips again and said, "Thank you, baby."

She headed out of his room, down the stairs, and into the garage; while Patrick followed her. She looked at his face and couldn't help but notice his sad expression. "Look, I'm sure this is hard for you, and if it makes you feel any better, you are my favorite guy. You were one of my first sponsors and someone I care deeply about. I just can't give you what you want, and if you can't allow us to be what we are, then maybe we shouldn't be anything at all."

"No!" Patrick quickly retorted. "No, it's okay. I can handle it. Just thought I'd remind you of how special you are to me. Know that I'm willing to do anything to prove my love, and I'll always be here for you."

Whitney smiled. "I appreciate you!"

When the garage doors opened, she eased out and drove quickly to her therapist appointment. The truth was Patrick wasn't just a sponsor; he was special. Of all the boys who had sponsored her, she had a deep connection to him. When they all came and went, Patrick stayed. She kept him around for many reasons. He treated her better than any sponsor or other boy, for that matter. He was the first and only to invite her to his home to meet his parents, and he gave her gifts on special occasions like birthdays and Valentine's Day. No other boys had ever done that. Although she would never utter the words "I love you," she had to admit that a part of her heart belonged to him.

Chapter Two

Whitney knew she was late, but since the doctor billed by the hour, as far as she was concerned, the only time wasted was her own. She knocked on the door and waited for an answer. She stared at Dr. Blakemore's shiny gold plate that was adhered to the door as she waited for it to open. What stood before her was not what she had expected to see. The brownish gold hair, hazel eyes, and fit physique caught her by surprise. The two therapists she'd seen previously were no comparison to the Bay Watch heartthrob with whom she was making eye contact.

"Hi, I'm Dr. Jake Blakemore, and you must be my very late one o'clock appointment."

When his lips parted into a smile, the brightness of his straight white teeth impressed Whitney even more. There was nothing worse than people with bad teeth, and she despised those who didn't practice good oral hygiene.

"I'm so sorry. Whitney Bonesteel." She held out her hand to shake his. "And I will never be late again." *You can bet your fine ass on that!*

"No worries, Ms. Bonesteel. It's a pleasure to have you here, even if you are a half hour late." He smirked. "Please, have a seat."

"Your office is nice. Did your wife help you decorate?" Whitney didn't see a ring, but she wanted to get straight to the point.

"Um, no. I'm not married—yet. However, this is the work of my fiancé. She's an interior decorator."

Whitney smiled. Although she was glad to hear that he wasn't married, she was a little disappointed to learn that he had a woman in his life. It didn't mean he would be impossible to get. It just meant it would take a little more work than she cared for.

"So, let's talk about you, Ms. Bonesteel. As you may know, I am a licensed sex addiction therapist. I've been in practice for over ten years and have done extensive studies on the matter. From my understanding, your parents encouraged you to come because they feel you could benefit from my services. Why is that?"

"I guess they think I'm addicted to sex," *Duh!* Whitney said in a matter-of-fact tone.

"Why would your parents think that?"

Whitney crossed her right leg over her left. She typically wore slacks, but on this day, she was glad she had settled on the skirt. She hoped the time she'd spent running track had made her legs somewhat appealing to Mr. Fine. "Because they found out I used to have sex with boys at my school, and when they'd caught me performing oral sex on the Gosley Twins during one of Mother's charity events, it caused quite the stir, as you can imagine."

"I see. Do you have an explanation as to why you act out in such sexual ways?"

"Well, from what I've been told, by past social workers and therapists, I do it to cope."

"Cope with what?"

"My feelings."

"Your feelings about ..." Dr. Blakemore prodded.

Whitney sighed. "Look, this therapy stuff ... I tried it before. The first woman told my mom everything I told her, so I cut her off for lack of confidentiality. The second one had an accent so thick I could barely understand what she said. So pardon me if I seem a little too disinterested in this." *Less my attraction to you.*

"Ms. Bonesteel ..."

Whitney was taken back by the formality considering her age, she wasn't even 30 yet. "Whitney is fine. I'm a vicenarian, not an octogenarian, for Pete's sake."

Dr. Blakemore chuckled. "Fair enough. Allow me to reassure you that whatever we discuss, whatever you decide to share, will never be spoken about outside of these walls without your permission. I promise you that."

I've heard that one before.

"It's called therapist-client privilege, and I take it very seriously. Okay?"

Whitney nodded, "Fair enough. So, to answer your question, I've grown up watching my parents use sex as a form of greeting. They meet people, they like them, they fuck them. Pardon my language. Although I've never seen Mother in action, I do know that's what she does, but I've seen Daddy do it. What makes them think I would be any different, when that's what they've exposed me to?" *He didn't need to know that my babysitter had taught me everything I knew about having sex for monetary compensation. I would keep that to myself.*

"Do you see anything wrong with your conduct? I mean, besides the fact that it's happened at school and during semi-public occasions."

Whitney thought for a moment. "Well, I guess the public thing isn't the most ideal or appropriate place, but other than that, it's my body and I should be free to do with it as I please."

"You are correct, Whitney. It only becomes a concern when you're doing it to fix, mask, or overcome certain issues in your life. Do you see any connection in your activities?"

"A little. Sometimes. I do notice when I'm having a bad day with Mother, I crave attention and interaction from the guys; or when Daddy upsets me and doesn't surrender to my wishes, I seek out sponsors."

"Sponsors?" Dr. Blakemore asked for clarification.

"Yes. That's what I call the boys whom I charge for sexual favors."

"Is it just males that sponsor you?"

"Yeah ... I've had fun with girls before. You know, do things with them to get a rise out of the guys. A few times, my two friends, Lina and Simone, and I charged all the boys in our economics class to watch us make out on Skype. They all gathered at one of their houses and we put on a performance for them. We each ended up with a hundred bucks that night. Can you believe it? Those few times were the only times I've been involved with girls."

"Mm hm. I see." Dr. Blakemore made notes. "Pardon my writing. I'm only doing this because it's our first visit, and it allows me to review the notes for clarity and reference. It's shredded afterwards. Okay?"

"No problem." Whitney was comfortable with him. Whatever he had to do so they could continue these sessions, she was all for it.

"When you engage in these acts, is money usually involved?"

"Most times it is. I don't charge because I need the money. I do it because it brings me satisfaction. To be honest, Dr. Jake, most of my sponsors are dorky, socially awkward, and are unfortunate looking, as mother would say. I have no interest or attraction to them beyond the transaction. I charge because it's easy money."

"Do you charge all men, or certain ones?"

"What do you mean?" Whitney asked for clarity. She thought about Jason, the boy from her grandparent's neighborhood and figured that's what Dr. Blakemore was referencing. "I used to be very attracted to guys that looked like me until Jason embarrassed me in front of his friends. He told them I smelled like rotten eggs between my legs and I got laughed at for a whole week. Since then I hated black boys, and now I only deal with Caucasian-looking ones."

"That's not quite what I meant. I guess I was trying to figure out if everyone you had sexual encounters with paid or just certain ones. For instance, what about the ones you *are* into? Do you charge them?"

Whitney looked away. She looked down and around his office. Her eyes settled on a piece of wall art. She loved paintings. Her mother was a good painter and she admired her talent, but that was about it.

Dr. Blakemore cleared his throat.

Whitney wasn't ready to answer such an uncomfortable question. "If they were into me, too, no, I wouldn't charge them."

"Are you saying there are guys you like but they don't like you?"

Whitney uncrossed her legs and then crossed them back, this time left over right. "That's happened before, or if they liked me, they only liked me when no one else was around." Except Patrick, he was different.

Dr. Blakemore picked up on her mood change. He heard the solemnness in her tone, witnessing the work that needed to be done. Whitney was masking, and it was his job to unveil her truth. “Would you like to elaborate on that?” he asked.

Whitney looked down at her watch. “No, not right now. Don’t you know it, we’re out of time. I got here late, remember?”

Dr. Blakemore looked at the clock on the table next to her chair. “We still have a little time.”

“Nah, we’ll have more at the next session.” Whitney stood and gathered her things. “Same time, same place next week?”

Dr. Blakemore nodded. “Yes, Whitney. Same time, same place next week.”

They shook hands and Whitney exited his office. She couldn’t tell if she was feeling good about the potential breakthrough or bad for needing to have one. What she did know was that Dr. Blakemore gave her all the feels, and her attraction to him was undeniable. He was the first therapist she liked, not just as eye candy but as a professional as well. For now, he served as mental healing. Later, she hoped he could give her sexual therapy. Plus, it helped that he was easy to talk to and seemed to genuinely care about her troubles.

The dual bonus was the reason she continued to go back and hadn’t cut him off as she had done with the others.

Anytime she was home on break, or needed an immediate intervention, she made an appointment to see him. But on campus, her best friend was all the therapy she needed.

Chapter Three

Jackson was a fancy man, with a big heart, bright smile, and a thing for the fellas. He and Whitney had grown close during their second semester of law school. Whitney typically kept to herself, but she was drawn to Jackson's energetic spirit. Lina and Simone are just as stuffy as she is, so it was good to meet someone with a more fluid personality. Every time they encountered each other, whether in passing or during class, Jackson would greet her with a broad smile and genuine eyes. But it was his consistency and directness that eventually won her over.

One day, Jackson had walked into class, sat right next to her and said, "Girl, let's stop pretending like we ain't gonna eventually end up being B to the FFs. You fly, I'm fly. I see you, and I *know* you see me!" He smacked his lips and used his pointer and middle fingers to connect their eyes.

The whole presentation caused Whitney to burst into laughter. "What makes you think that?"

"You special. I can tell. You strut your cute, bourgie, mocha-colored ass into class every day and watch these white boys salivate over you and act like you are none the wiser."

But Whitney wasn't acting, she secretly hoped one of the cute boys would crush on her and ask her out like they did the rest of the girls on campus, but that wasn't her reality. "First, I don't act like anything. Second, I'm not bourgie!"

Whitney had been hearing that all her life and, quite frankly, she was tired of it. It wasn't her fault she was taught to master her walk, cross her legs, and arch her back while sitting before she could talk. Those were her mother's teachings and when in Bethany's presence, Whitney could never be a child. She had to be a mini-version of her mother.

What she liked most about Jackson was that he always called her out on her crap. If she was being too stuck up, he let her know. "Hunty, we are at a *party*. People laugh, dance, and twirl at parties. Loosen up!"

If she was behaving too recklessly, he told her. "Now, no one likes to have a good time as much as me, but that is your third line and we have exams tomorrow. I need you to show up binge-free and ace them shits, uhkay!"

Most importantly, he never judged her. He allowed her to be herself at all times. And when she witnessed him not being his true self, it made her uncomfortable. It was those kinds of talks that sold Whitney on her new friendship with Jackson.

Whitney had just pulled up to a familiar spot preparing to service a sponsor when her phone began to ring. She took note of who it was and ignored it, with intentions on calling him back. When it rang again, she answered.

"Jacks, what is it, I'm kind of busy?"

"Girl, Shon's in labor, can you take me to the hospital?" Jackson had just gotten a call from his mom letting him know that if he wanted to see the baby born, he needed to get there immediately.

"Right now?" she questioned, thinking of the money she was about to make.

"Yes, now, my mom said I don't have a lot of time."

"Ugg I guess," Whitney reluctantly agreed. "You're interfering with my money and it's going to cost you big time!" She hung up and headed straight towards her best friend.

When they arrived at the hospital, Jackson went to his sister's bedside, while Whitney sat in the waiting room of the Labor and Delivery unit.

Two hours later Jackson came running into the lobby, screaming in excitement, jolting Whitney from her sleep. "It's a boy! It's a boy, Whit! Now, I have a niece *and* a nephew," Jackson squealed with sheer elation. "C'mon, I want you to meet them!"

Whitney wiped her eyes and mouth to rid the evidence of her deep slumber. "Okay, okay. Lead the way." She tossed the blanket that was draped over her body onto an empty chair, ran her hands down her face, and followed Jackson to the delivery room. They arrived just as the nurse was walking out.

The nurse was firm but polite. “She’s going to be tired and will need some rest. We still have to do some tests on the baby, so not too long, okay?”

Jackson nodded in agreement and dragged Whitney into the room. “Hey, sissy. I’m back. I want to officially introduce you to my B to the FF that I’m always talking to you about.” Jackson placed his hand on Whitney’s back, pushing her forward. “Whitney, this is my twin sister, Roshonda, my mother, Opal, and my two-year-old niece, Quayvianna. And this is our newest addition, Quazier,” he shrieked happily.

“Nice to meet you” echoed in the room as the family greeted Whitney.

Whitney moved closer to the bed, where Roshonda was holding her new blessing. “He’s absolutely gorgeous. Congratulations!” Whitney said to the new mother of two. She walked over to Jackson’s mom and shook her hand. “Pleasure to meet you as well, Mrs. Opal. Jackson has told me so much about you all.”

“Oh, the pleasure is all mine. Glad that law school is serving him well and he’s making friends.” She eyed her son. “Rohan, I see your fashion has changed since you’ve been in school.” She looked him over with apparent disapproval. “Seems to have changed *a lot*.”

Whitney raised her brow but kept quiet. She silently observed the dynamics between Jackson and his family. Jackson's niece seemed to adore her uncle. Ever since they'd entered the room, she had been glued to his side. She also noticed how protective of him his sister seemed to be.

Roshonda spoke up. "I like it, Ma. I think he looks good. Happy, peaceful, you know." She seemed to be the only one in the family who accepted Jackson's sexuality. According to Jackson, his father and brothers were much more critical than his mom.

Opal scoffed. "If that's what you see. Seems a bit flamboyant to me."

Whitney squirmed in discomfort. She had just witnessed, firsthand, the shaded insults Jackson must've had to endure all his life. She adjusted her posture in her seat and looked away from his mother, hoping it was a respectful indication that she didn't appreciate the snide attacks on her friend.

"My style has changed a bit, Mama. I'm finally growing into me. I understand that may look different for y'all, but it fits who I am."

"And who exactly is that?" Opal prodded.

"Mama, can you please see if the nurse has another blanket? I'm a little chilly," Roshonda asked, trying to steer the attention away from her twin brother. She'd known Rohan was gay since elementary school. She was also aware that the rest of her family knew it, too. They just didn't want to accept it.

When Mrs. Opal left the room, Roshonda turned to her brother. "Don't mind Ma. You know she's always opinionated. I love the new look and persona of *this* Rohan. You keep slaying, brother!"

Although Jackson seemed to appreciate his sister's comments, Whitney could tell he was bothered by the exchange with his mom.

Whitney peeked at her wrist and took note of the time. "I'm famished, best friend. I haven't eaten all day. Wanna grab a bite?"

Jackson looked at his sister. "Sis, you okay if I step away for a few?"

"Of course. I would say bring me something back, but I haven't been cleared to eat yet." She grimaced.

"Sucks to be you." Jackson tilted his head to the side and pursed his lips. His mother entered at that moment, and he straightened his face and neck. "Mama, you want something to eat?"

"No, I'm good." Her response was short, almost rude.

Whitney waved to Shon and Mrs. Opal and left the room with Jackson. Once they made it to her car, she mentioned what had been on her tongue since leaving the hospital. "Jackson, I normally don't tell people what to do, but since you 'keeps it all the way real' with me," she said, mocking his lingo, "I'm going to be honest with you. The Jackson at school is way different than 'Rohan' around family. You're not your bubbly self. When your mom is around, you seem to put on this front that I've never seen before."

Jackson dropped his head, nodded, and smirked. "You *would* see that. After all, you get to see the real me on campus, which I hide from my family." He paused. "With the exception of my twin sister, my family denounces homosexuality. All my life, I've had to hear 'fag' this and 'fag' that, and 'I'd kill that mf-er if he ever approached me.' When I realized I was one of those people they hated, I had to decide quickly if I was going to stand and be ridiculed or worse. Once I got tired of hiding who I was, I decided I had to leave in order to live as the real me. As soon as I graduated high school, I left home. I was homeless for a few months before I decided that the best alternative was college. There, I can get an education, shelter, food, and hopefully meet some great people ... like you."

"I wouldn't say I'm great," Whitney admitted, thinking of all the ways she had been selfish and self-centered.

"Girl, stop. You *are* great! I am living my best years because of you. You've taught me to stop worrying about what other people think. Fuck the world and be myself. After we met, I started dressing different, walking taller, and living unapologetically. Now, I'm a divo," he said and snapped. "I even started going to gay clubs. Can you believe it? Even sucked my first dick, chile! Girl, you taught me so well that his ass started stalking me!" As if on cue, his phone started ringing. "Look, that's him calling me now. He probably tryin' to get it in before he has to get home to his wife. He hasn't exited the closet yet, Jackson joked. "Since meeting a couple of weeks ago, we've only met face to face twice. He said he's been curious for a while and until now, he's stuck to porn. I gave him head and now he wants to try it on me," Jackson smirked.

Whitney burst out laughing. "Now, that's what the hell I'm talkin' about." She gave him a high-five. "Where do y'all meet up at?"

"Tonight he wants to meet up but don't have a lot of time, so I'm going to be waiting by his job, so we can get a quickie in before he gets his wife from work."

They walked inside the restaurant and placed their orders. Once they were seated, Jackson said, "Seriously, had it not been for you, Whit, I may have never lasted this long. It's hard finding your identity and securing your place in life. Thanks to you, I genuinely feel like I have someone I can trust, learn from, and be open with, without any judgement. It's like nothing turns you off. I could tell you I just got banged in a sewer pit, and you would ask me how it was. I could tell you I had a train ran on me, and the only thing you'd wanna know is if I got mine!"

"Eh ... but don't say 'nothing turns me off,'" Whitney interjected. "I don't do pedophiles, gerontophiles, or animals. That's where I draw the line. Other than that, I lack morals, Jacks. I perform nude for those who are sexually deprived, I sleep with other people's spouses. I seduce random men and have even befriended their wives just so I can have the upper hand. I prey, I plot, and I profit. That's how I get ahead. I lack love and loyalty. Everyone in my life serves a purpose, and when that purpose is no longer served, they're disposed of."

That was Whitney's ugly truth. She was nothing like her parents, who were cautious of what they said, how they spoke, and behaved. That took too much effort for Whitney. If she couldn't be herself around certain people, then she chose not to be around them. She had resolved, long ago, that she wasn't going to change who she was just to please others. She would change her environment before she let it change her. When the judgement, whispers, and sneers started coming from those closest to her, she walked away and never turned back. Even her two other closest friends, Lina and Simone, were victims of her detachment. That was only because they still rubbed elbows with the same snobs her mother entertained during her uppity soirees — like the upcoming one she was dreading —that they didn't even realize they were being kept at bay. So avoiding the snobs meant sometimes avoiding them. That distance opened the door for Jackson to fill a social void.

“First of all, what you doing with all that money you makin’?”

“I’m saving most, spending some,” she said.

“And exactly how are you saving it? You just can’t be making large deposits in your bank account. Unless, of course, you tryin’ to have the alphabet boys after your ass.”

“Well, I only deposit hundreds at a time, and some I keep in my dorm.”

“Girl, are you stupid or just plain dumb? Your dorm is the worst place. You know my old roomy had all his money confiscated because he couldn’t show legitimate proof of how he got it?”

“I heard about that and that’s because he was selling weed on campus. I’m not selling drugs.” Whitney sneered.

“No, boo boo, but you *are* selling ass. And since both are illegal, all they need is a little birdy to whisper in their ear, and you know you’ll be next.” Jackson pursed his lips in condemnation. “But this is what you do. You create a business, register it with the proper channels, open a business account, and make small, regular deposits. Make sure you keep ledgers, so if you’re ever audited, your shit will be tight and right!” Jackson snapped his fingers for effect.

“But how am I justifying the payments?”

“Hold ‘*fun*raisers,’ duh! We can host passion parties, and instead of selling toys, you do your thing and send them home with little trinkets, or some shit. Collect your money and make them deposits, chile."

Whitney thought for a moment. "Jackson, you are a fricking genius."

"No, I'm not. I'm just sharing what I've learned in my classes. Business law is my thing. Criminal law is yours. I keep the IRS off your ass, and you keep the feds off mine." The two of them laughed.

Whitney and Jackson headed back to the hospital. When she pulled up in front to let him out, she placed the car in park. "Are you going to be good? I can either come back to get you tomorrow or send for you."

"No, I'll be fine. I don't have class on Fridays, so I'll just catch a bus back." Jackson stood to hug Whitney.

"Thanks, B to the FF, for driving me and meeting my family. I love you so much."

"Anything for you, Mr. Jackson. Make sure you call me up as soon as you get back on campus!"

Although she may have wanted to hear all about his night, she was planning to have a spicy one of her own.

Chapter Four

Whitney awoke to total silence. She checked the alarm clock on the side of her bed: eleven a.m. Jackson would have woken her up already had he been back from his visit. She pulled out her phone to check her emails, texts, and call log, and saw that he had, in fact, called and texted her late Thursday night, after she had dropped him off at the hospital. She'd heard her phone vibrating when she was with Patrick but never bothered to answer it. The text was a selfie picture, with a caption: "About to get me soooome."

She smiled and immediately dialed his number. When she didn't get an answer, she left him a message. "Geesh! I know you were busy, but I at least expected to hear from you afterwards. Call me back! Miss you. Bye."

Before performing her morning routine, Whitney checked the online tracking and confirmed that the package she'd sent to Roshonda was delivered to the hospital, which made it even stranger that she hadn't heard from Jackson. *He definitely would've called to thank me or given his sister my number to do so,* she thought.

Whitney flossed, brushed her teeth, and took a quick shower. She threw on a sweat suit and headed to class. It was an important lecture and she couldn't risk being late from trying to track Jackson down. However, as soon as class was over, that would be the first thing she would do.

Three hours later, Whitney walked briskly back to her building. Her ringing cell phone reminded her of her post-class task. She retrieved her phone from her back pocket and expected to see Jackson's number. Instead, it was her father.

"Hi, Daddy," Whitney answered with a tinge of disappointment.

"Hey, Skittles. Guess who's in town and wants to treat his princess to dinner?"

"Ooh, Channing Tatum?" Whitney mused.

Her father sighed. "You wish. Will you be free at five?"

"Yes, I'll be free. I just finished an exam. What are you doing here?"

"Well, I have to take care of some business for Ma and Pa. And I ... I have to address something else."

"Like what?"

"Just some stuff, Skittles. I'll share more at dinner, okay?"

Whitney gave him a curt reply and disconnected the call. Lately, her dad had been moving in stealth. He'd always been a classified kind of guy but not to this degree and not for seemingly unofficial things. She had no idea what he was hiding, but if he wasn't honest with her about whatever it was, she was going to begin treating him the same way she treated her mother—cold and distant.

Without closing out the dial screen, she placed another call to Jackson and, this time, the phone went straight to voicemail. The vibes were off. Something wasn't right. Whitney couldn't place her finger on it, but she knew something was up. She had an hour before she had to get ready for her date with her dad. She used that time to search for Jackson. She went by his room, but there was no answer. She used the spare key he'd snuck and copied for her to look inside. Besides some new semi-nude dude posters, there was nothing different, or off about his room.

She took note of the bags that contained the new outfit he'd planned to wear to a campus party. She saw a shoe box opposite the bed and a couple of hats he must have tried on prior to choosing the fedora he'd worn the night they went to the hospital. *Such a divo.* On her way down the hall, she ran into a few people who were familiar with Jackson. Each reported that they hadn't seen him the past couple of days.

Whitney returned to her half-packed dorm room. It was their last semester of law school so she decided she would prepare for life off campus. She had entered a bid on her first piece of property and had plans to share her new digs with Jackson. She had applied to several local law firms and was confident she would hear back from one of them. She threw her school bag on the floor, sat on her bed, and searched for the number to the hospital.

"Patient Services. How can I direct your call?"

"Hi, uh, my name is Whitney Bonesteel. My friend's sister gave birth there on Thursday, and I want to see if she's still there?"

"The name, please."

"It's Roshonda Jackson. She was on the third floor."

A few moments passed. "There's no one here by that name, ma'am. Are you sure you have the name right?"

Whitney became annoyed. "Are you sure you spelled it right?" she shot back but then realized she wasn't even sure she knew the correct spelling of her first name.

The operator matched her sass. "Well, unless there's another way to spell Jackson, I'm sure I did."

Whitney sighed deeply. "You're right. Thank you." She hung up.

She realized Jackson and his sister probably didn't share a last name if his sister was married. *Shit!*

Whitney began rubbing her neck and chest profusely, just as she did every time she grew anxious. *Think, Whit, think*! She searched the Internet again, typing in Jackson's full name and hometown, his mother's full name and town, and anything else she could think of to try and get contact information for someone who may know the family. Her searches either yielded too much or nothing at all. *Where's a private investigator when you need one!*

A ding came through her phone, indicating she had a text message. It was from Patrick, telling her he missed her already. She replied with a simple "Thank you."

She kept the web browser open so she could resume her search for Jackson later and brought her phone to the home screen. A glance at the clock by her bed revealed it was time to meet with her dad. She took another shower and threw on some black slacks, a collared blouse, and a blazer before heading off to their favorite spot. Frederick was a distinguished man and would never approve of his daughter wearing streetwear in public, so whenever they met for their occasional face-to-face encounters, she made sure she looked her best. She needed her dad's help finding her friend, and her attire proved she meant business.

~ ~ ~

"Daddy!"

Whitney stood when she saw her father walking toward their table and greeted him with a hug. They met at the same restaurant and sat at the same table each time he came to visit her at school.

"Skittles!" he replied. Whitney's dad held on to her tightly and placed a kiss on her forehead. "How's Daddy's special girl?"

"You normally say *only* girl. Is there someone new in your life you aren't telling me about?"

"My baby, always so keen. I tell you, you always find a way to confirm that I am making the correct investment in your future. You are going to make a fine attorney, sweetheart."

"Thanks, Daddy! I guess I'm taking after the best."

Frederick had graduated cum laude from Harvard and made partner at one of the most prestigious political law firms in the nation; now working hard to become a judge. Even though he was proud of her, she felt blessed to be his offspring.

The waiter came to take their orders and Whitney did her best to avoid his face. He was someone she was very familiar with and didn't want to let on to her dad just how acquainted they were. Her father opted for black coffee and she ordered a glass of the best wine in the house along with their usual meal: lamb chops with garlic mashed potatoes and seasonal veggies.

When the waiter walked away, Whitney clench her thighs remembering their night together before she spoke. "Well," she asked again, "who's the lucky lady?"

Frederick sat quietly for a moment, taking in the exquisiteness he'd created with his first wife before speaking.

"Before I get into all that, your granddad told me to tell you hello. He said he misses you and wishes you would call or visit."

The waiter returned with their drinks, and Whitney took a sip from her glass. "How's Nana?" she asked.

"Nana's not doing too good, Skittles. The doctors seem to think she may not be able to remain home with Pa too much longer. The dementia is making her combative and she's become increasingly physical with Pa. It's just not a safe environment anymore."

"Well, what are they saying? Are they making her go into a nursing home?"

"No, sweetheart. They can't make her, but they are strongly encouraging it, which is why Pa asked me and my siblings to come meet with the doctor. Today, we all agreed they will go into a continuing care community, where they can still be together, but Pa can get some outside help to assist Ma. That way, he'll have respite from being her primary caregiver and resume some of his favorite hobbies. With me living southwest and my brother and sister living so far away, it's hard for us to have a pulse on exactly what's going on." He took a sip of his coffee. "You know, Pa has a black eye from Ma being aggressive when he tried to shower her?"

Whitney winced. "Oh no, Daddy." She lowered her head in shame. She began to feel some remorse for distancing herself from her grandparents. "As the oldest grandchild, I could be a little more present in their lives. I mean I'm about to be twenty-five, and I haven't seen them since the beginning of law school. It's just that the last time I visited, the vibes felt off, so I didn't bother to go back."

"Skittles, I just think the timing wasn't good. Ma had just gotten diagnosed, which was hard for her to accept. Pa was miserable after they got the news. I'm sure they meant well. It's still no reason to just stop reaching out. I know you got the packages Ma sent."

Whitney nodded slowly. "Yeah, I did." Her heart grew sad. She did miss her grandparents. She'd lived with them for most of her childhood. And even when she'd returned to her mother so she could "be educated in a better school district" than what Albany had to offer, she still threw fits until her mother drove her back down the Northway so she could spend her weekends and school breaks with them. At least there she had a sense of family life. Plus, she liked the fact that she was exposed to more people who looked like her. That was until the horrible night her Aunt Valene's crazy boyfriend showed up. Whitney still vowed to get revenge on Mitch, but she shook the thought from her head, refocusing on her immediate priority.

"Daddy, can you help me?"

"Of course, sweetheart. Whatever you need."

"I have a friend. I think he may be in trouble." Whitney recapped the story about Jackson up until moments prior to their meeting. “That’s so out of character for him. I’m worried that something happened, but I don’t want to assume.”

“Of course. A friend of yours is a friend of mine. Send me everything you know. I’ll have my secretary look into it.”

“Thanks, Daddy!”

The waiter set their plates in front of them and asked if they needed anything else. They both shook their heads and he walked off. The paper under her plate caused her to smile.

“Looks good doesn’t it? Her dad asked, assuming the food made her happy.

She nodded. “So, what was it you had to address?” Whitney asked.

She watched as her dad stared at her lovingly and chewed his food. She could tell there was something he wanted to say but he was hesitant.

“Nothing, Skittles. Let’s just enjoy our meal.”

Although Whitney obliged, she knew better. He had something on his tongue, and he may not have shared it now but, eventually, he would. She was sure of it. For now, she just needed help locating Jackson.

Chapter Five

Sunday morning was dreary. Whitney had hoped to get all her packing done, so when she got the clear to close, there would be nothing left to do except purchase furniture. She checked her phone and although there was nothing from Jackson, she saw the email icon at the top of her screen and was pleased to see that it was from her dad's secretary. It contained contact information for Jackson's family. She contemplated calling the number for Mrs. Opal, but figured she would check Jackson's room one last time before reaching out.

She took a quick shower and decided to stop by his dorm before running a couple of errands. She drove to his quad and parked in the lot closest to the door that led to Jackson's side of the building. It had now been two full days since she'd last seen or spoken to him, which was the longest they'd ever gone without contact since meeting three years ago. When she got to the floor of his dorm, she walked down the hallway that led to his room. To her surprise, the door was open and Whitney wasn't sure if she should be happy or upset with him for ghosting her for as long as he had.

"Jackson, I should beat your—" she began as she walked into his room.

But Jackson wasn't there; instead, his twin sister, Roshonda, and a man she'd never seen before both turned to look at her.

"I'm so sorry. I thought Jackson was back. Where is he? I've been trying to get ahold of him since Friday." Whitney watched as Roshonda's eyes watered. She looked from her to the man and back to her.

"Whitney, come sit down," she said.

"No, I'll stand. Where's Jackson. Is he okay?" She knew he wasn't, but she had to ask anyway.

"Jackson, he ... Jackson is dead," Roshonda said with emerging tears.

"What? No way! When? How?" Whitney's breathing increased. She grabbed her chest, her neck, patted her chest again. "You're kidding right?"

Roshonda shook her head. "No, I'm not. He was killed sometime late Thursday night."

Now, it was Whitney's turn to shake her head. "Killed? Nah, not Jackson. He was a great guy. No one would hurt him."

"I know he was, but that didn't stop whoever did this."

"So, the person who killed him hasn't been caught?"

"No, the detectives are following up on leads. We think whomever he linked up with that night may have been the one to hurt him. He left the hospital and said he was headed to meet with someone and would grab some last-minute things so I could bring the baby home the next day and …" Roshonda broke down.

The guy she was with wrapped her in his arms. "Hi, I'm Roman, the twins' older brother."

"Hi ..." Whitney's voice cracked. She looked at Roman. "Is he, is he really gone?"

Roman nodded. Whitney saw him look around at the posters on Jackson's wall and then back at her. She wanted to protect her friend's image, defend his dignity. He would have never been comfortable with his mom or any of the men in his family seeing this side of him.

"Those are mine." Whitney snickered. "I put them up yesterday as a joke to let Jackson know I had been in his room and was thinking about him." She turned to look at the large poster. "He would have laughed so hard and called me to tell me how crazy my 'bourgie' ass was."

Roshonda composed herself. "I begged my brother to bring me here. I was hoping to find some clues as to who may have done this. The detectives said it seemed personal because of how he was assaulted and …"

Roman interjected. "We were just hoping to find whatever we can to help with leads."

Whitney didn't want them snooping too long, for fear they may find something of Jackson's that they shouldn't. She gave them the key to his mailbox and suggested they check that. While they were gone, she went under his bed and removed the photos of naked men he kept in a shoe box. She then went into the bottom drawer of his desk and took out all the letters he had received from interested partners. She also went to his closet, looked in the left pocket of the third vest from the back wall, and removed the paper that contained the passwords to his phone, dating sites, and his social media account. Once he realized how trustworthy and nonjudgmental Whitney was, he let her in on the most protected parts of his life. He always said, “Girl, if I ever die in my sleep, make sure you delete this and throw that away,” and they both would laugh. Now, Whitney couldn’t hold back the painful realization that his plan had come together too soon.

Roman and Roshonda returned with a stack of mail. “A lot of it was junk mail, but he does have a few items from the registrar and financial aid,” Roshonda stated. “I’m just going to take it back home, so we can go through it there.”

“We just walked in seconds before you, so we didn’t get a chance to search in here,” Roman added.

“I apologize. I don’t mean to pry. We became very close a few years ago. Your brother was a true friend to me.” Whitney felt tears forming. “I’m really sorry for your loss, and I’m going to miss him … a lot!”

Roshonda walked over and hugged her. “I know this must be hard on you, too.”

Whitney let a few tears drop and quickly wiped her eyes. Emotions were for the weak, and she couldn't be seen in such a vulnerable state.

"Oh, and thank you so much for the basket! I got it yesterday morning. The hospital called and told me I had a delivery, but there was no number, so I couldn't call to thank you."

"You're very welcome. If it's okay, I'd like to give you my number. If you ever need anything, please don't hesitate to call."

"That would be great. We're just about done with finalizing the funeral arrangements. Once everything is confirmed, I can share the details with you if you'd like," Roshonda offered.

"I'd like that very much," Whitney said. "I'll get going so you two can have some space." Whitney grabbed ahold of Roshonda's hand and gave it a squeeze.

She waved bye to Roman and slowly released Roshonda's hand as she walked out the door. As soon as she got back to her room, she turned on the shower so the temperature was as hot as she could take it. She got in and cried for her friend. Once she felt like all her tears had washed down the drain, she got out. She spent the next few hours going through the images of his social media accounts. Instead of deactivating the accounts, she deleted all messages and "friends" who would signify his true lifestyle and left the account active so his loved ones could visit the page from time to time. All profiles on dating sites were deleted. But without his phone, there was nothing she could do with the content it contained.

The next day she got a text from Roshonda letting her know that the funeral would be that coming Wednesday and she included the address for the services. Whitney had mental funerals for people all the time, but this was her first real funeral, the first time she had to say farewell to someone she genuinely liked, which didn't include a lot of people.

A part of her wanted to call Patrick for familiarity and comfort, but recently he'd let it slip during a conversation that he was interested in taking their relationship to the next level, and asked about her ring size. She told him she wasn't ready, not only because she wanted her freedom, but she had committed the ultimate betrayal by sleeping with his dad. Ever since then, she'd been avoiding his calls and ignoring his texts.

Whitney sent a coded text to her dealer to let her know she was stopping by. After purchasing her usual quantity, she contacted one of her sponsors and headed toward East Mass. She hoped the white substance and some good sex would help her forget about her problems, if even for a moment.

Chapter Six

If she wasn't on top of her studies and her grades, Whitney was convinced she would score low on the bar exam. The burden of losing Jackson and having to take such an important exam was too much for her to bear. She spent most days studying and crying and most nights drinking and drugging, trying to block out the emptiness in her heart. When she really felt down, she reached out to Shon, and the two of them would spend hours talking about Jackson and sharing stories. Jackson was their common denominator, and being in each other's presence, was the medicine they didn't know they needed. Since the funeral, they had grown just as close to each other as they had been to Jackson and had begun to spend a lot of time together.

As Whitney sat in front of the mirror, putting the finishing touches on her makeup, she delicately bopped to the music in the background. She and Shon had been to the mall earlier and purchased an outfit for her mother's gala. She decided to get the new color palate Mac had just released and was excited to wear it tonight. She was casually enjoying the sounds of Pink's new album, when the music stopped.

"Girl, can we like play some Mary J. Blige, or Faith Evans, or Total, or anything but this shit!" Shon sighed.

"Um, I happen to like Pink. She's a great artist."

"She might be, but she is *not* putting me in the mood to attend this party."

"Trust me, this isn't your average party. My mother is hosting a fundraiser for Saratoga's first mayoral candidate of color. There's going to be a lot of pale folks with deep pockets, sipping dry-ass champagne and eating bland appetizers."

Shon fell back on the bed and huffed. "Girl, what are you getting me into? I just want to hear some good-ass hip-hop and R&B music, sip a stiff drink, and gawk at some good-looking bruthas. You *do* know it's been over a year since I last had some dick, right?"

Whitney turned around and looked at her friend, who, at the moment, held an expression that mirrored her twin brother's.

"See, that's why I miss Jackson. He wouldn't be complaining like you are. He'd be singing along with me and sipping some dry champagne until I was ready."

Shon tossed a pillow at Whitney and watched as she ducked. "Well, I'm not Ro*han*. I'm Ro*shonda*, and we have different tastes. But whatevs. I'll be a good sport."

"Good. Do you like my new makeup?" Whitney asked. She turned her head in different angles.

Shon gave it a long overview. "I mean you do a great job with the application, but I hate the foundation. It's too light for your skin. You need something that matches your tone more. You have a beautiful milk chocolate complexion. I wish you'd show it off. That makes you look ashen," she answered honestly. "Plus, you don't even need that shit, anyway. You should be natural, like me." She laughed. "Other than that, it looks good."

Even with the compliment, Whitney's self-esteem plummeted. It was just another example of the internal struggles she'd been facing for the last twenty-plus years. She was too dark for the whites and lights and too "white" for the blacks. She couldn't seem to catch a break.

"Whatevs. I like it." She put on her blouse and shoes and announced that she was ready.

By the time the two of them arrived at her mother's, she could tell by all the cars that the event was in full swing. She pulled into the circular driveway, got out, and handed her keys to valet. She looked over her car as she waited for Shon to exit before they walked to the front door. Although she was grateful that her parents had bought it as an eighteenth birthday gift, she wanted something new and more extravagant. She was confident the connections she would make tonight would be the come up she needed to purchase her dream car.

Once they got inside, Whitney could tell by the looks of the décor that Bethany had spared no expense. The bottom of the silk drapes kissed the floor, traveled up the wall, and looped across the ceiling. Tall white columns were strategically placed throughout the foyer and grand room. Servers walked the floors, while others were stationed near the entrance and offered beverages and an array of hors d'oeuvres to newcomers as they arrived.

Whitney accepted the fuchsia colored bubbly concoction and raised it to her lips. She turned to Shon. "You have to get this," she said.

She sipped a second time and made eye contact with her mother. Bethany gave a subtle nod and resumed speaking with the couple who had her attention. Whitney smiled at those she was familiar with, spoke to those she admired, and was tight lipped with the ones she didn't care for. Her mother received a combination of the three as she made her way over to Whitney.

"Hello, dear." Bethany leaned in to greet her daughter with a formal embrace.

"Mother."

"Nice of you to come," she half-smiled, "and bring a guest."

"If it's a problem, we can go." Whitney partially turned toward the front door and pointed at it. The tone in her voice alerted those within earshot that something was off. Whitney knew what it was. It was her mother's vibe.

"Of course not." Bethany stared at her face. "Honey, did you change your makeup? I liked the lighter shades you wore before. It softened your skin." Bethany peeked down at her midsection. "And cut back on the pasta. You look thick in the waist," she stated. "But no, please stay, mingle, eat, but not too much, and enjoy!" Bethany air kissed Whitney on both cheeks, nodded at Shon, and proceeded to greet others who were just arriving.

The sliver of respect the mother and daughter held for each other was about as shallow as the depths of the love between them. She didn't think she and her mother would ever see eye to eye. At this point, all she could ask for and give was cordiality.

Her two friends from school spotted Whitney and made their way toward her.

"Bethany still trippin'? Lina asked with an Italian accent.

"Yeah. She seems so ... so *Bethany*," Simone added.

Lina, Simone, and Shon had all met at the celebration of life Whitney had organized at Jackson's dorm room, so there was no need to familiarize them with each other.

Shon noticed that Whitney wasn't feeling the topic, so she changed gears. "You mean to tell me all these folks are rich?"

Whitney giggled. "Damn near. And if they don't have money, they're married to it." She winked. "Feel free to mingle." Whitney smiled at Shon and gestured toward the crowd. "I have to do some scouting myself." She walked off, leaving the three ladies to talk amongst themselves.

A lot of familiar faces were in attendance, several of whom she recognized from television or because they'd been to events her mother had thrown before. Some, she remembered very well, others she chose to forget. She spotted the makeshift bar in the far corner of the room. As she headed in that direction, someone caught her eye, someone she didn't want to see and desperately hoped to avoid. Whitney did an about face and headed toward the left side of the house, where one of the isolated bathrooms were located. Once inside, she closed the door, collected her breath, patted her face, and rubbed her chest. She walked toward the sink and placed her purse on the counter so she could rummage through it.

Focus, girl, focus! Secure a sponsor or two, get the hell out of here, and ignore him. Ignore him, ignore him, ignore him.

Whitney found the piece of paper she was looking for. She began unfolding it until the pure white powder was visible. Using the straw that was lying next to the small mound, she placed the tip at her nose and inhaled. She did that once more before throwing her head back in euphoria.

The bathroom door opened abruptly. It was *him*.

"So, you're just going to ignore me?" Jack asked.

Whitney glared at his face through the mirror as she rapidly refolded her product and placed it back into her purse. “Are you stupid?” she hissed. “You have to be! Why the fuck would you follow me in here?”

Jack stood in the doorway, “Listen, I just need a minute. You stopped answering my calls. Stopped returning my texts. He needs answers!” He said in a hushed whisper.

Whitney inhaled deeply and turned to face him. “If you don’t get the hell out of here, *you* are going to need to come up with answers. I can’t do this. *We* can’t do this. Your son loves me, and I’m not capable of loving him the way he deserves.”

“I know. I’m not here to convince you to go back. Just call him, please. Patrick just wants some closure, he’s going crazy. Tell him you’re not ready to settle down and you don’t feel you’re wife material.”

Whitney huffed. “I can’t believe you just said that. Maybe I *would’ve* been wife material, had his kinky-ass father not convinced me to make him my slave bitch—”

“Lower your voice!” he commanded with a stern whisper. Jack nervously looked around to make sure no one was close by.

Whitney ignored him. “After all the times you begged to go down on me, knowing your son had just been inside of me, play ‘massa and winch,’ let me spank you until you passed out, or asked me to stick *my* fingers in *your* ass because it helped get your dick hard, all while hiding your nasty fetishes from your wife—and *I'm* the one who's not marriage material?" Whitney chuckled. "I can't believe this shit. How about you give your son the answers." She gathered her things.

Unbeknownst to them, Jack's wife had been in search of him and as a result, heard most of the exchange but didn't realize it was her husband in the mix. She had made it to the door just as Whitney turned the corner. When she saw who walked out after Whitney, she shrilled loudly.

Chapter Seven

Damn! Whitney didn't want to cause any ruckus. *How was I supposed to know there were people right outside the door?*

She sought out her friends and spotted Shon and Lina talking to a guy near the fireplace. She briskly walked in their direction.

"We need to get out of here!" she whispered in Shon's ear.

Shon turned her head toward Whitney and scowled. "Nooo, we just got here! Plus," she leaned in closer to her friend, "I think I see some serious eye candy. You know I be on my Bradley Cooper shit sometimes."

Whitney could see that her friends were enjoying themselves and, although she didn't want to interfere, she also knew things were about to turn ugly. The voices got louder as the crowd parted like the Red Sea. She could see Patrick's mom walking toward the front door, crying loudly and scanning the room.

"Where is that whore bag!" Jack's wife yelled, spittle flying from her mouth. "Where is she?" Mrs. McNapis yelled one last time before storming toward the door.

Whitney used the throng of folks standing on the tips of their toes to witness the action as a shield while she ducked into the crowd. When the coast was clear, she went to get her drink.

The crowd was at its thickest, and Bethany decided it was time to start the artwork auction. Everyone interested in bidding was provided a paddle. A knockoff Georgia O'Keefe painting started the process. The onlookers ooh'd and aah'd and mentioned how the flower had "such opulence" and appeared "full of fertility." To Whitney, it looked like a vagina, and she wished someone would say it.

Drawing after drawing, some way, somehow, Whitney was able to correlate the piece to sex. After all, art was abstract. But the fourth to last image caught her eye and the unfamiliar name of the painter caught her ear.

"The bidding is starting at five thousand. Do I have five thousand?" Bethany petitioned.

A few paddles went up, including Whitney's.

"Do we have fifty-five hundred?" Bethany asked. "Five thousand and five hundred to the man in the blue striped tie. Six thousand?"

Another paddle up.

The bidding went up to nine thousand, and Whitney was still in the race. Her friends gasped. They knew she had money but not enough to be spending on pricey, unnecessary artwork.

Bethany thought the same thing. Her eyes threw darts at her daughter and her voice nearly cracked. “Nine thousand. Do we have ninety-five hundred?” Relief crossed Bethany’s face when the man in the blue striped tie raised his paddle.

Whitney raised hers again at ten thousand, twelve–five, and fourteen thousand. She showed her displeasure when the man in the blue striped tie outbid her at fifteen thousand. She turned around and looked in his direction, only for him to give her his back, which irritated her more and heightened her curiosity. Her realtor had just informed her that her bid on the condo was accepted, and the piece of artwork by the unknown artist would’ve been her housewarming gift to herself.

Methodically and cautiously, Whitney inched further into the room, headed toward an angle that would allow her to get a solid view of his face. As slick as she tried to be, he was even slicker. If she was only two angles off on the right, he would engage with someone to his left, thwarting her progress at each step.

Her efforts were interrupted when her mother’s long-time bridge buddy tapped her on the shoulder to say goodbye. The two of them exchanged pleasantries and wished each other well. As soon as she walked off, Whitney turned and looked side to side.

The man with the blue striped tie was in front of her. “I see we share a similar eye.”

Whitney cleared her throat. “I guess so.” She looked intently at his face. *What is he doing here?*

He removed his right hand from his pants pocket. “Good to see you.” He smiled.

She extended her hand.

“Feelings aren’t mutual, I see.”

“They are. I’m just curious as to what you would be doing at my mother’s event.” She held onto his hand. “Are you two friends?”

“I wouldn’t call us friends. She sent an invitation to a friend of mine, who extended it to me. Since the future missus is trying to expand her business, I thought it would be a good opportunity to network while supporting diversity and inclusion in the political world.”

Whitney eyed him suspiciously, recalling how she had fired her other therapist for being friends with her mother. “I told you I didn’t want my parents involved in any of my personal dealings.”

“And I also told you, Ms. Bonesteel, that I take the privacy of my clients very seriously. Well, since I haven’t seen you in a while, I wonder if I can still consider you a client.”

His statement was weighted, at least to Whitney. Her attraction to him was not subtle. His acknowledgement of the long break since their last session was suggestive. His presence at the event was telling.

When she didn't answer, he spoke again. "What did you like about that painting?"

Whitney walked to the bar to get a refill. He followed her.

"It had gravitas. A hint of romance with a tinge of erotica, if that makes sense."

Dr. Blakemore tried to hide his pleasure behind an ambiguous smirk. "Interesting."

"And you?" she asked.

He pondered her inquiry, made eye contact. "It's like craving love, hating love, wanting love, and needing it all at the same time."

Whitney eyed him sideways, impressively confused, cautiously intrigued, undeniably stimulated. Her nipples hardened. He took notice through the sheer material of her fitted blouse that was neatly tucked into a high-waisted A-line skirt. His adams apple shifted with a hard swallow.

Whitney could feel her body heat rise as the moisture between her thighs increased. Sex for money had become routine. The big-face bills got her in the mood. Rarely did her partner make her horny, but Dr. Blakemore did. She clenched the thickest part of her legs together and rotated her neck slightly.

Whitney looked down, and when his eyes met hers, she gestured for him to follow her, and he did. But when she walked in one direction, he discreetly walked in another to throw off any inquiring minds. They met up at the back staircase and he followed her to a room. When he entered, he pulled his shirt up and unbuckled his pants. His petruding member confirmed their intent. Just as he pulled a foil wrapper from his pocket, Whitney produced one from her bra.

She stepped into him, grabbed a handful of his manhood, and whispered in his ear. “Wear mine!”

Normally, she would be in control, as she would want to get the rendezvous over with as quickly as possible. But with the looks Dr. Blakemore gave her, she wanted to see just how well he handled his business. She didn’t have to undress to prepare for their experience, when he lifted her skirt; he would find she wasn’t wearing panties.

Once he got the condom on, she placed one leg on the nightstand and waited for him to enter. The fullness of his erection felt good inside of her. She massaged her love button to increase the wetness. Whitney worked her Kegel muscles to squeeze him as he slid in and out of her. She continued to play with herself until he grunted and then pulled out. Whitney watched as he stroked himself, emptying the remaining fluids into the condom.

“There’s a bathroom down the hall on your left,” she told him. She grabbed her clutch and walked into the bathroom located inside the bedroom.

The fact that the sex hadn’t quite matched his looks or his size, was a little disappointing and a bit of a turn off. *We can work on that, though,* she reasoned. Now that they had crossed that line, there was no way she could continue to see him for mental help. It was now time she found another therapist. However, unbeknownst to him, he was about to become her new sponsor. A man who could afford to spend fifteen thousand dollars on a painting, was a man she needed in her life.

Chapter Eight

After Whitney and Shon left her mother's party, they stopped by the cemetery to visit Jackson's gravesite. Whitney wasn't the one to show much emotion, but seeing Shon break down over the loss of her twin brother caused her to shed a few tears as well. They told him stories and expressed how much they wished he was there. They made a couple of promises, shared some laughs, and endured more tears, all the while consuming a fifth of scotch they had purchased earlier that day. Although the alcohol and lines may have given Whitney the perk she needed to maintain her energy the night before, it caused her to be extra tired the next morning. That's why when her cell phone started ringing and it wasn't even nine a.m. yet, her first thought was to let it go to voicemail, but she quickly thought better of it. The last time she'd ignored a call was the night Jackson died and she vowed, no matter where she was or what she was doing, to never ignore another call, especially from the important people in her life.

"Hi, Daddy," she answered groggily.

"Hey, baby girl. I really need to talk to you. Can you make time for me today?"

"Yeah, sure. Everything okay?" Whitney was concerned.

"Uh, yeah, baby. Everything is okay. Daddy just needs to talk to you about something important."

"Okay, you coming to my dorm or..."

"Let's meet at the restaurant. I think I'll have a drink with you today."

"Okay," Whitney responded suspiciously. Her father never offered to have a drink with her. Being that the end of the semester was nearing, she figured he wanted to celebrate with her, but wasn't sure; so she asked. "Daddy, what is this about?"

"Just some stuff, Skittles. I'll share more at lunch, okay? See you at one-thirty."

Whitney gave him a curt reply and disconnected the call. Her gut was telling her something wasn't right, but she couldn't figure out what it could be. She and her dad talked about almost everything, but now it appeared he may have been keeping something from her. She performed her daily hygiene routine and decided to head to the furniture store to pick out some things for her new place before meeting with her dad. When she arrived at the restaurant, he was seated in their usual spot, nursing a glass of dark liquor.

"Hey, Daddy!" Whitney greeted him with a kiss on the cheek.

Her father stood and pulled out her chair, waiting for her to sit, before sitting back down. A glass of the restaurant's best wine was waiting for her. "Hey, Skittles!"

Whitney watched as her father's head lowered and he took a long sip from his snifter.

"Baby, Daddy has something to tell you. I've wanted to mention this to you for some time now, and I almost told you last time we were here, but I ... I just couldn't bring myself to tell you."

"What, Daddy? What is it? Are you getting divorced *again*? Did your wife catch you cheating? You're in love with another woman? It's always something with you," she remarked in jest.

Frederick looked at Whitney, his eyes pleaded for her to forgive him for what he was about to share. "No, none of that, baby girl. It's ... well ... um, you have a sister."

"A sister?" Whitney asked in disbelief. She took a sip from her drink as she waited for further explanation. "How, when? Daddy, don't you think you're too old to be having babies. You should have pulled out. You know Mother always swallowed hers. I don't even know how you got me in," Whitney half-joked.

"That is way out of line! Please don't speak that way about your mother, Skittles. I know you two don't always get along, but she does love you."

Whitney looked up at her dad. “Daddy, Mother never loved me. She loved the security she received because of me. Being pregnant by you meant you would marry her and she could live the lavish-wife life she always wanted. Let’s face it, her half-white bastard-child of a mother taught her well.”

“Whitney, for Pete’s sake, watch your mouth! That is still your mother and you best give her the proper respect she deserves,” he commanded.

Whitney rolled her eyes. She’d just barely finished her glass of wine and was prepared to order another once the waitress returned to their table. “Yeah, whatever.” She brushed off his remarks. “About this little sister of mine. When am I going to meet her? Do I have to fly all the way across the country to do so?”

“No, that’s not necessary. She lives right here in Albany.” He looked at her just in time to see her brows furrow in wonder. “And she’s not little.” He looked away. “She’s your age.”

“My age? How the fuck is she my age and we’ve never met?”

“Can you please watch your mouth? We are in public, and you’re a young lady. Behave that way!” he chided.

“*You* are telling *me* how to behave in public? How many times have you gotten caught with your pants down and only because of your clout were your scandals swept under the rug?” Whitney scoffed.

“Lower your voice, Whitney!” He was upset. Rarely did he call her by her birth name. “Here me out. I had just found out your mother was pregnant with you, so I proposed to her to let her know I was serious about our relationship. Well, prior to that, I wasn’t too faithful and had been sleeping around with a woman I’d met at Subway. Two months before you were born, your aunt Valene told me a friend of hers knew a woman who had a child who looked like me. I sent Valene to look into it, but the woman denied it was my baby, so I didn’t think much of it. Fast forward about two years later, and the woman came back to the campus, looking for me but I had transferred schools. We did a court-ordered paternity test and it came back positive.” Frederick looked down at his drink and back at Whitney, who was waiting for him to continue. He sighed. “By then, I was so terrified to tell your mother for fear she would leave me and take you away that I didn’t say anything. Over the years, I’ve tried getting in touch with the woman, but she wouldn’t respond. Your mom and I got married and, eventually, I let it go. But Ma and Pa didn’t. They kept trying to reach out and hounded me to do the same but …”

“What’s her name? Where exactly does she live?” Whitney quizzed. She didn’t want to hear the excuses. She wanted answers. “Matter of fact, what are your plans for her now? Is she going to be inducted into the family? Will she be included in everything we do? Where does she fit into *our* lives, Daddy?”

His eyes shifted. “I’m not sure sweetheart. I do want her to be a part of the family.”

Whitney shook her head in disbelief. A part of her wanted to be happy she had a sibling, but the other part of her felt betrayed. She wished this had come up much sooner. “Why now, Frederick?” Whitney tended to call him by his first name when she was seconds away from being dismissive.

Her dad sighed deeply. “Please, don’t call me that. I’m still your dad, Skittles.”

“Yeah, and apparently someone else’s, too.”

“Sweetheart, look at the bright side; it’s not like you have to share your toys or bedroom.” He forced a smile he hoped she’d accept.

“Nope, none of that. Just my father, his heart, his time ... his *estate*. Shit!” Whitney shook her head. “Twenty-four years, Daddy!” The more she thought about it the angrier she became. “You’re telling me you knew I had a sister for over twenty years and didn’t bother to mention it until now?”

Patrons in the upscale establishment began peeking at them as her voice escalated.

“Skittles, please. This is just as hard on me as it is you. If I had let your mother find out, she would have taken you and left. I couldn’t risk that! Plus, with Ma’s illness, I thought about reaching out to her so she could meet the family before something happens.”

Whitney tipped the wine glass to her lips to drain the last of its contents. “So, you’re okay with losing me now?”

“No, of course not. I—” He stopped, realizing what she had said. “Baby girl, please. I’m sorry I didn’t tell you sooner.”

Whitney removed the cloth napkin from her lap and tossed it on the table. “Yeah, I am, too, Daddy.” She stood, “I am, too,” and walked out on her father.

She didn’t know what upset her more, the fact that she was no longer an only child or that she was just finding out. Although the answer to that riddle may not have been clear, it had created a new wound, one that required immediate numbing before it surfaced too much. Today was just one of those days when all she wanted to do was be alone. No phone, no friends, just her, her vices, and her music.

Chapter Nine

With school behind her, Whitney was glad to be free from the confines of the educational correctional system. She always felt like the only difference between law school and prison was the freedom to come and go as she pleased. Otherwise, she was at the mercy of her studies, and the professors were no different than correctional officers, who often dictated what she could and couldn't do.

Graduation was in two weeks, and she had thought long and hard about inviting her parents. Even though they had been the ones to fund her education, she really didn't feel like they earned the right to see her walk across the stage and receive her degree. *Screw them!* She sent the tickets to Lina and Simone instead. Shon would be there as well, as she and her family would accept Rohan's honorary degree in commemoration of his anticipated accomplishment. That was all the support she needed, so every time her father sent her message asking for the details of the ceremony, she told him she didn't know yet. To her surprise, they had found out anyway and showed up.

Graduation day came and went, and now it was time to decide what she was going to do moving forward. Whitney stopped by the campus to check for mail. She was surprised by the stack of letters both she and Jackson had received from potential employers and called Shon immediately.

"What you doing?" she asked as soon as Shon answered.

"Feeding Mr. Man and playing tea party with the junior missus. Why, wassup?"

"Jackson and I got letters from prospective employers. I wanted to read mine but was hoping to have someone with me. Can you meet me at the sandwich shop on Central Ave.?"

"Sure can! Give me an hour to get the kids together. See you in a few," Shon said and ended the call.

Once they arrived at the café, both ladies ordered a half sandwich and soup.

"Jackson and I always came here to eat. He liked it because he got to see all the cute, buff guys who entered and left the gym." Whitney pointed across the street as she headed to their favorite section of the café. She let Shon sit first. "That was his favorite seat, too!" She smiled at the memory.

"Guess it's twin shit," Shon said. She watched as Whitney pulled a stack of letters from her expensive handbag and took note of her solemn expression. "So, you want to go first?"

"Nah, you can," Whitney offered.

She handed Shon Jackson's mail and watched as she opened envelope after envelope. There were five letters, and every agency had offered Jackson an opportunity.

Shon became emotional. "He was really excited about this one." She held up a letter from the board of directors at the LGBTQ Center in Downtown Albany. "He knew there was a lot of discrimination surrounding the LGBTQ community, and he wanted to do whatever he could to help change the laws." She sifted through a couple more. "And this was his second choice, an opportunity to work at the Albany County District Attorney's Office in their financial crimes unit. He always said that since Albany is the capital of New York, it would be easier to lobby for change. A lot of legislation was created here, and if he was going to have an impact, he had to be where it originated."

Whitney smirked. That sounded just like the Jackson she knew. She looked at her stack and held it up. "See these? These are all the places my daddy suggested I pursue. He knew, with his solid name and my good grades, there was no way I could be denied." Whitney held Shon's gaze. "But screw these." She ripped the letters in half two at a time. "If I accepted these, that would be me doing his work. It's time I do something that would benefit someone other than myself." She paused, lost in her thoughts.

"What's up with you? You've been so moody and distant the last week or so. When I call, you don't answer but will text me to see what's up. You didn't even acknowledge your parents at the graduation. Talk to me. What's going on?" Shon asked with genuine concern.

"My dad told me I have a sister."

"Oh, shit! Congratulations, Whit!"

"Congratulations, nothing. She's not a newborn, Shon. She's the same age as me, like a few months older."

"Oh." The smile faded from her face as she sat back in her seat. "I can tell you're not happy about it, but having a sibling is a good thing."

"I know it should be and maybe if I'd found out sooner, you know, a long time ago, I would be happier. Now, it just feels like a stressful burden. My dad's trying to get me to embrace her but I'm not emotionally ready for all that."

"Why, though?" Shon asked.

Whitney explained to Shon what she'd said to her dad about having to share him.

Shon reached over and grabbed ahold of Whitney's hand. "Listen, I just lost my bother and would do anything to have him back. Having siblings is the best feeling in the world. They're like the best friends God picked for us. I don't think it's such a bad thing, babe. I know you're not feeling it right now, but take some time to think about meeting her. If she's anything like you, I think you'll love her." Shon offered a smile.

"Yeah, maybe you're right. I'll think about it."

"What's her name? We may know of her already and don't even know it."

Whitney sneered. "You know, I don't even know. I asked my dad, but he never answered me. Now, I'm not sure if I want to reach out and ask him again, or find out on my own. I'm still upset with him."

"Well, whatever you decide, I'll be right there to support you. I'm sure you'll do the right thing. You know I'm your new B to the FF, right?"

Whitney let out a long, hearty laugh. "Once you're finally exposed to the real me, you might head for the exit," she warned.

Shon threw her head back in laughter. "If *that* Ro could handle you, then *this* Ro can, too." She pointed at herself.

Whitney wasn't so sure that Shon knew what she was getting herself into. She seemed to be the homey, family-oriented type, and Whitney was a whole other breed. College had only made her much more vicious in her pursuits. Although Whitney may have been willing to share some stuff with Shon, she felt she needed to keep other things close to her chest. Shon was cool and seemed open minded, but Whitney knew better and had been disappointed in the past by those she trusted.

Chapter Ten

Jackson's death, finishing school, passing the bar, moving, and work may have kept Whitney occupied, but it damn sure didn't distract her from the fact that her father had a whole grown kid in this world, whom she'd known nothing about until weeks ago. And the more she thought about her feelings, the clearer it became that she didn't want to accept her. Whitney was her daddy's girl, his grown princess, his favorite bag of Skittles in human form. *Why couldn't it be a brother?* she thought. Not even her father's women could hold a torch to Whitney. She was the reason a lot of her father's relationships didn't last. If Whitney didn't like his lady friends—and she didn't care for any of them—she made sure their lives with her dad was a living hell. She either made them hate her so much they'd moved on, or she played her daddy like a pawn until, eventually, he left the relationship. Even Bethany was jealous of how tightly Whitney had her father wrapped around her finger.

Whitney had dedicated a lot of brain muscle to this situation. She thought back on old conversations, past actions, and former interactions. She honed in on a few instances when, even at a young age, she could sense the tension in the room. One day, her aunt Valene had come home, and as soon as she'd entered the house, she ran past Whitney in search of her parents. Whitney recalled hearing whispers and "Oh, my Lord! How can we get ahold of her? Can we see the baby?" Now, she realized that was when her father's secret had been unleashed or confirmed. She remembered one time she had gone shopping with Nana and Pa and was allowed to pick out whatever special toy she wanted. After Whitney had chosen a doll, her nana bought two of them, but couldn't express why when seven-year-old Whitney had asked. Then there was the time when she saw Nana writing letters and placing checks inside the envelopes before sealing them. Each time, she would place the letters in the nightstand drawer next to her bed. That memory prompted Whitney's unannounced visit to her grandparents' home, not far from where she had to report for work.

She parked on the street, just before the driveway, feet away from the for sale sign posted on the lawn. Whitney checked her reflection in the visor mirror before stepping out of the car. It had been years since she'd last checked on her grandparents and a part of her felt guilty that the visit was more self-serving than genuine.

Nana's suggestion that her father should have placed Whitney over his lap a long time ago and gave her "a good spanking" was partially what had kept Whitney away for so long. Even if she wanted to blame herself for her lack of sincerity, she had to admit that her parents would rather shut her up with gifts and accommodations than some good ol' fashioned discipline. It wasn't that Nana wasn't right, but in her daddy's eyes, she did no wrong, and Whitney wasn't okay with anyone trying to distort his image of her.

When she reached the front door, she rang the doorbell once and then knocked. She was greeted by a man who was once of great stature but now appeared weathered and fatigued.

"Hi, Pa." Whitney smiled.

"Skittles! Hot damn. Well, I'll be." Her grandpa reached for her and brought her in for a big hug. "I can't believe you came to visit. Come on in here, so your nana can see you." He moved aside so she could enter. Once she passed the threshold, he closed the door.

"Mable, Mable!" he called out to his wife. "Guess who's here?"

When he didn't get a response, he turned his attention back to Whitney. "I think she's probably in the bathroom. Let me go check on her. Have a seat. Make yourself comfortable." He walked toward the back of the house.

Whitney listened for his footsteps, and once he was far enough away, she walked to the left of the living room to see if their bedroom was still located there. It was and she saw that the nightstand was in the same place. The thought of being so close to finding out the identity of her nemesis of a sibling caused her hands to sweat. She rubbed her neck, then her chest, and patted her neck a couple of times. The anticipation was getting the best of her. Rather than delay any longer, she opened the top drawer of the nightstand. Before she had a chance to move anything around, she heard her grandfather's voice.

"Skittles, baby, you still in there?"

"Yes, Pa. I'm still here."

"Okay, she's coming. I'm just helping her finish up. We'll be right there."

She gave the top drawer a thorough inspection before checking the bottom drawer. She lifted things and moved them aside but found nothing.

Damn, damn, damn! Where would an old person hide stuff? she wondered. Whitney looked under the bed and between the mattress and box spring but came up short.

"Now, who you say is here again?" she heard her Nana ask.

"You'll see soon enough. Now, just come along, Mable. The girl looks like she's headed to work."

Their steps were getting closer. Whitney felt like she had waited too long. She could see that they'd done a lot of decluttering since she'd last been there, more than likely, in preparation of the sale of the house. She looked around one last time before heading back to the living room. Good thing she did. On her way out, she spotted a small box with what appeared to be several pieces of mail inside. There was no way she could leave without inspecting that box, but first she had to play the role.

"Hi, Nana! Did you miss me?" She opened her arms and greeted her father's mother, whom she hadn't seen in almost four years.

Getting to that box full of mail before she had to report to work would be difficult, but Whitney was determined to do it. Her Pa had gone to the kitchen to get a cup of coffee for her Nana and while he was gone, she seized her opportunity.

"Wow, Nana! Looks like you guys are all packed. This thing looks heavy," Whitney commented as she walked over to the box and opened it. As expected, multiple letters were inside but none with a name or address. *Shit!*

Chapter Eleven

When Whitney made it to work, she placed a quick call to her father's office and got his secretary on the line.

"Hey, it's me, Whitney. Is my dad available?"

"Hey, Whitney. No, he's not. Is there anything I can help you with?"

"Actually, yeah. I'm trying to pay him a surprise visit this summer and wanted to invite his other daughter." *That sounds too informal and suspect.* "Well, my sister, and he forgot to give me her name and address. Would you happen to know that?"

"Oh, um, you must be talking about the one who's about to graduate with her criminal justice degree."

Realizing he had been talking to his secretary about his other daughter, Whitney was upset, but she didn't let it keep her from finding out more information. "Yes, that's her."

"He's so proud of you both. He's never mentioned her by name, but he did say she was attending the College of St. Rose in Albany."

"Wow! He didn't even tell me she was about to graduate! That's great!" Whitney scowled.

She thanked the secretary for her time and made her promise not to ruin her surprise by telling her father she'd called. Whitney was familiar with the College of St. Rose. A few of her sponsors went there, and they all thought her name was Jasmine. Now, all Whitney needed was a face for her father's other daughter, so she'd know who she was looking for, and she'd be well on her way to meeting someone she already knew she didn't like.

The work day was a blur. All Whitney could think about was the possibility of coming face to face with Frederick's unveiled offspring. As soon as she left work, she headed over to the campus for a visual inspection. Without a name, her only hope was facial recognition, and she knew that wouldn't be hard. There weren't many black girls attending the school, and if his daughter had any of their father's features, picking her out would be easy.

Whitney parked in the lot across the street from the entrance and watched as people came and went without a care in the world. She sat in her car, mustering up the nerve to get out. *What if I see her? Do I speak, play dumb, or tell her who I am? Nah, I can't tell her that. She might think I'm crazy. But what if she's really nice?* Whitney continued to go back and forth with her conscious before finally counting to ten and getting out.

Her red fitted pants accentuated her full bottom and the cotton t-shirt highlighted her breasts. As she walked in front of a parked car, the sound of the horn caused her to jump. She grasped her chest.

"I'm sorry. I didn't mean to scare you, beautiful," said a handsome Latino man. "My friends call me, Chench, and I just couldn't let you walk past me without saying hello."

"You startled me. I thought I did something wrong." Whitney managed a smile.

"Nah, you did nothing wrong. And your parents did everything right." Chench said, looking her up and down approvingly.

Whitney chuckled at his compliment. *Damn, he's kind of cute!* "I'm Whitney. Nice to meet you."

"The pleasure is all mine, pretty lady. You got a man or a number?"

Patrick crossed her mind. He had been her closest thing to a boyfriend, but she'd never committed. "Actually, no. No, I don't have a man."

"Let me change all that. Can I get your number?" he asked again.

"Sure."

Just then, a girl whose complexion matched Whitney's and was just a tad bit shorter stepped between them and started in on Chench. "So, is this the reason your ass can't get me on time?"

"Oh, shit! What's up, Shy? I was just asking her where I could find you," Chench lied.

Whitney furrowed her brows in confusion. She wasn't sure if she should walk away or stay and watch the exchange. The woman was visibly upset.

"Whatever, Dominic! She wouldn't know. If you wanted to know where to find me, you should've picked up your phone and called me. Speaking of which, where is your phone? Because I called and you didn't answer."

Dominic? He just said his name was Chench. Whitney moved a little to the left so she could get a better view of the girl. From the side, her features mirrored her own: slender nose, with a slight flare at the nostrils, full lips that accentuated her dimples. *Could it be?*

"It's in the car, charging. Why you all tight and shit? I'm here, ain't I?"

"Yeah, but you're late, as usual."

After watching the two of them go back and forth a few times, Whitney grew tired of the exchange. "I guess I'll let you go. I don't want you to get in trouble," she said to Chench.

"Trouble? Please, I'm good!" Chench stated, trying to sound tough. "She ain't my mother."

"Oh, word?" the girl he called Shy shot back. "Are you serious? Fuck you and that bitch—"

Oh, no she didn't just call me out my name. "Bitch? Who are you calling a bitch? Because the only—"

Before Whitney could finish her statement, Shy had hauled her cell phone at Whitney's face, hitting her right in the mouth. It hit the ground and broke.

"What the hell did you do that for?" Whitney yelled, holding her mouth.

"Oh, my bad. That was for him," Shy quipped. She walked off and Chench followed her.

Whitney wiped her lip and tucked it inside her mouth to stop the bleeding. She glared down the street at the two of them and did her best to etch the girl's face, shape, and size into her brain. Her gut told her she was Frederick's daughter, but she needed proof, and she wasn't going to stop until she got it.

Chapter Twelve

The first full week on the job left Whitney feeling like she had chosen the gig from hell. Of course, she would have been better off pursuing one of those fancy firms her father had lined up for her. Had he not dropped a bomb on her, she may have gone along with his recommendations instead of pursuing one of Jackson's passions. Now, here she was, bombarded by cases that contributed to overbooked dockets, when her real interest was white-collar crimes. That's where she had excelled in school and gotten the most satisfaction. Getting justice for the LGBTQ community didn't appeal to her. She wanted to bring down the big fish, the "untouchables," those who walked and talked like their shit didn't stink and hired big, fancy lawyers like her dad to protect their illegal interests. Those were the ones she wanted to bring to justice.

The workload, coupled with toxic colleagues, had Whitney moody all week. However, Mother Nature had played a part as well, and now that her cycle had run its course, she wanted to enjoy her weekend, no matter what it entailed. She had just agreed to settle on community service for a transgender man who had vandalized a store after being denied service by the homophobic clerk and was now faced with additional cases. She headed to the restroom, and when she was done, she grabbed a paper towel from the pile on the counter and threw it away after drying her hands. She grabbed ahold of her rolling file cabinet and headed back toward the courtroom. As soon as she walked in, she was bombarded by her clients' family members.

"Ms. Bonesteel, make sure McGregor gets bail. I got that cash. He good!" someone yelled. "Get Moniker ROR'd, man. This shit been going on too long," another one called out.

Whitney ignored their statements and continued to the reserved attorney area. She wheeled her rollaway next to her and proceeded to pull out her cases for the day. The first one up was a twenty-two-year-old Hispanic male: criminal possession of a weapon, with the intent to cause harm. That was just one of many more cases to mitigate.

When it was time for the judge to enter, the bailiff announced, "All rise!"

Those in the courtroom remained standing until the judge spoke. "You can be seated. Is counsel ready to proceed?"

"We are, Your Honor," both attorneys answered.

The defendant walked in front of the judge and the bailiff swore him in.

"The defendant is being charged with unlawfully brandishing a weapon and threatening the victim with bodily harm. Does the defendant understand these charges?"

"Yes, Your Honor," Whitney replied.

The judge turned to the prosecutor. "I understand you've reached a plea?"

"Yes, six months in an anger management program and one year probation," the prosecutor replied.

"I can't believe we're accepting this. He tried to kill me!" the transgender client whispered to Whitney.

"I know, but because it was only a threat and there was no physical harm done, that's the best offer. It *does* give you some justice. Do you really want to take this to trial? It'll be long and drawn out and you'd be risking a harsher sentence."

Her client shook his head in defeat. "No, I guess not."

"Counselor?" the judge said.

"Yes, Your Honor. We accept the plea offer." Whitney looked at her client, who was clearly unhappy with the plea.

"Sir, how do you plead?"

"Guilty," the defendant replied.

That went on for ten more cases. Eight pled, one was adjourned, and the eleventh defendant refused a plea. He declared his innocence and wasn't going to accept anything other than a dismissal, and Whitney couldn't blame him.

She packed up her briefcase and saw a handwritten number lying on top of one of her files: "Call me some time." A local phone number was beneath the note. She looked up and the bailiff was looking back at her, giving her a delicate wink. Whitney raised her brow at him and walked off. She was horny and needed a high, but she wasn't desperate. Maybe if he was seventy pounds lighter, three shades brighter, and five inches taller, he would've had a chance.

As she placed her briefcase in the trunk of her car, her phone rang. "Hey, Shon." Whitney was happy to hear from her.

"Hey." Shon's tone was flat, and it was clear that something was wrong.

"What's up? Everything okay?"

"Besides missing my brother and the police not finding the person who killed him, yeah, I guess everything is okay." Shon grew silent, and then the sniffles started. "I miss him so much. He was truly my best friend. We entered the world together, and although I knew we wouldn't leave together, I didn't expect that he would be gone so soon."

Whitney let her friend vent. It was good for her to release her pain and anger this way rather than vigilante justice or self-medication. Any time Whitney felt down, she packed her clothes and her vices and went far away from her problems.

"You know what, let's go on vacation. Summer will have come and gone before we know it, and I haven't been finalized plans to go anywhere yet. Jackson promised he'd accompany me on my next trip, so I think we should go together instead and have a good time in his honor."

Shon perked up a bit, but reality hit quickly. “I wish. I can barely afford to pay myself no mind, let alone go on a vacation. Plus, with a new baby, I wouldn’t feel right. But you still should. I’m sure Jackson would be right there with you.” She smiled at the thought.

“Okay, well since you can’t do a trip, you should come visit tonight. I’m pretty much done unpacking most of my things and I’m almost settled into this condo. My furniture was delivered a few weeks ago, and I could really use a hand hanging curtains and pictures,” Whitney proposed.

The silence let her know Shon was thinking. “Let me call you right back.”

Whitney had made it only two blocks before Shon was ringing her phone. “I’ll see you in a few hours. Mom agreed to watch the kids!”

Whitney smiled. Shon’s personality was the type of energy she needed. Lina and Simone were great company, but they were stuffy and proper and reminded her too much of where she came from. But not, Shon. She was fun, funny, outgoing, and so down to earth. She was just the company Whitney needed after a long day.

Chapter Thirteen

Club scenes weren't really Whitney's thing, but she knew Shon liked them. When Whitney wanted to be social, she typically went out of town or linked up with one of her paramours for a private shindig at an exclusive location. All she really needed for a good time was coke, cock, and scotch on the rocks. But this weekend would be different. She had convinced her friend to come visit her and she was determined to show her a good time. Plus, she wanted to unwind. As much as she tried to make her father's illegitimate child a non-factor, it became a big deal. This new addition meant everything she thought she would be the sole beneficiary of, would now be split in two, and that was too much reality to bear. Whitney knew she was being selfish, but she was okay with that.

Whitney and Shon entered Club Truce in Downtown Albany and as soon as they stepped inside, the smell of weed, cologne, and cheap body spray permeated her nostrils.

"Shit!" Whitney yelled to Shon over the music. "And this is appealing to people?"

"Girl, some of these folks are regulars. Party every weekend with the same faces at the same places." Shon looked around.

Whitney's face said everything she was thinking. "I wouldn't be caught dead in a place like this. Not my thing at all." She followed Shon to the bar.

"Well, how do you party?" Shon asked as she maneuvered through the crowd.

Whitney gave her a contemplating glance. "If you're around long enough, you'll see." She smirked.

When they made it to the bar, Whitney ordered drinks for them both and stood close by, people watching. It was a little after one in the morning, and there was no way she could spend another minute in that place. The later it got, the sketchier the people looked.

"Girl, hurry up with that drink and let's go somewhere else," she told Shon.

"Okay. There's this other spot one of my homegirls used to bartend at. We can go there."

The two ladies placed their empty cups in the trash and proceeded to leave the club.

"Where y'all going? The party just getting started," one of the bouncers called out to them. Shon flashed a smile and shrugged, while Whitney kept walking. She didn't do black men. The one time she had, she was ridiculed and vowed that her kind wasn't for her.

Whitney got the directions from Shon and began driving. She excused herself and reached past the passenger seat to open the glove box. She took out an eyeglass case and removed its contents.

"Oh, *that's* how you party!" Shon teased.

"Partially," Whitney answered. "You indulge?"

"Nah, not my thing, but do you." She held up her hands. "I'm judgement free. Plus, I used to smoke before I got pregnant. Weed is more my speed."

Whitney made a mental note of that. When she came upon a red light, she snorted a line. Shon used that time to search the radio for the station playing the best music, but Whitney's ringing phone stopped her.

The number was private. "Hello," she answered skeptically. There was no response. "Hello," Whitney said again. When the person on the other end didn't reply, she hung up.

Shon found the local station and was glad they were playing her kind of music. She noticed it was an artist she liked and turned it up. "Yasss! Now, this is my shit!" Shon sang along to Jon B's newest record. "Times like this, I wish I wasn't breastfeeding. A nice clip would be so amazing right now."

Although she had smoked weed at times, Whitney and her friends chose powder, as it was more of an upscale drug. Weed had too much going on. It stunk up your clothes, breath, home, and was lacking the discretion they'd come to appreciate about coke.

She joined Shon in the singalong and bopped her head.

"He can sing his ass off," Shon said.

"He can sex his ass off, too."

Shon looked at Whitney, smiled, and nodded before turning her attention back to the outside. As if just catching on to what Whitney had said, she turned back to her. "Wait, did you just say he can fuck?"

Whitney smiled. "Yup."

"You fucked Jon B?" Shon was incredulous.

Whitney laughed at her remark. "Yes, we were intimate. Jackson was with me. We went to New York City for an event, and he was performing. I got us into the lounge where he was making an appearance. I used my charm to get close to him and did what I do best. He liked what I was saying, so when he left, he made sure I left with him."

"Get the hell outta here! Jackson never told me that! Well, shit, you know anybody who knows somebody who knows Memphis Bleek?"

"Memphis Bleek?" Whitney gave her a questioning look. "Girl, he is 'hood as hell."

"Yes, Bleek! That muthafucka is foine. Just my type: dark, handsome, 'hood, and talented. Mmm! I don't wanna cuff him or nothing like that. I just want one night, girl. Just me, him, and opportunity." Shon squeezed her legs in anticipation.

Although Whitney didn't see what she saw, she was amused by Shon's confession. "I have a lot of connections. I may be able to pull something off for you."

"Word?" Shon was excited by the thought.

Whitney nodded.

"Damn, my brother was right. You dat bitch!" Shon wasn't sure if that was okay to say. "I'm sorry. I hope I didn't offend you."

"Girl, no. I've been called way worse. Plus, it's not the content; it's the context, and I felt the love." She winked to let her know it was all good.

Whitney had other things to be concerned about, and being called a bitch by someone she knew meant no harm wasn't one of them. She had to preserve her get-back for her father's other child.

~~~~~~~~~

Whitney pulled into the parking lot and found a spot toward the far end of the building. After another line she placed the powder back into the glove compartment and proceeded to the door with her new B to the FF beside her.

The doorman of the club was taking his job a little too seriously. “Sorry, it’s after one a.m., and we not letting nobody else in,” he bellowed.

“It’s barely one,” Shon snapped, correcting him.

He pulled his cell from his jacket pocket and looked at the time. “Like I said. No one after one.”

Shon sucked her teeth and cocked her head to the side, ready to sass the doorman, but Whitney stepped in.

“Listen, we’re not here to violate rules, cause any trouble, or be a burden. I just graduated from law school and my friend just had a baby. We’re just out trying to have a little bit of fun,” Whitney explained sweetly.

The bouncer eyed them both. After a few seconds he spoke, “Twenty each.” Whitney paid the fee and he opened the door and moved aside. “Enjoy your night, ladies.”

Shon nudged Whitney and smiled at her. “I’m impressed!

“My Nana always said you get more bees with honey than you do with shit and by the way you tilted your head, I knew it wasn’t gonna be sweet.”
~~~~~~~~~

Shon led the way to the bar and Whitney offered to pay for the drinks.

"I'll take a White Russian. Running to the ladies' room. Be right back." Shon walked off.

Whitney observed the club and the people. Although it wasn't what she was used to on the rare occasions she did step out, she instantly noticed that it was a more mature environment than the place they'd just left. The bartender approached her for her order. After giving her the details, she crowd watched again until her drinks were placed in front of her. Right when she was about to grab it, her phone rang.

"Hello?" She could barely hear over the noise in the background. Once she saw Shon, she motioned to the drinks and walked toward a quieter area before she spoke again.

"Whitney?" the caller said.

"Yeah. Who's this?"

"It's Patrick!"

The sound of his voice caused a stir of emotions. *Should I hang up, stay on the line, or get it over with?* She had been ducking him for a while now and, frankly, she was tired of it.

"Hey, Patrick. What's up?" Whitney sighed.

"You know what's up. You slept with my father?! How could you do that to me?"

Whitney knew, at some point, she was going to have to address the situation between them, but she didn't expect to be doing it now, at this hour in the morning.

"Look, it's late. I'm tired and I—"

"Tired? Are you kidding me? It sounds like you're at a goddamned concert, and now you're tired? No! I am not hanging up with you until you give me answers. I had plans to marry you, and you do that to me." His voice was shaky yet stern.

Whitney knew this wasn't the time or the place and she also knew there was no way she could admit to the man she *almost* considered marrying that she had done more sexual things with his father than she had with him.

"Patrick, I can't, okay? I just can't. If you want answers, please ask your dad." Whitney hung up the phone and vowed to change her number.

She walked back to the main room and searched for Shon. Whitney spotted her talking to a guy near the front of the club. "Hey. Sorry about that. Where's my drink?"

Shon picked it up from the table and handed it to her. Whitney removed the napkin that Shon had placed over it before taking a sip. She looked at the man Shon was talking to and almost choked. *Chench!*

When Chench made eye contact with Whitney, she smirked and looked away. She wasn't new to life and could clearly see that Shon was enjoying whatever Chench was saying to her. Every time he leaned in to whisper in her ear, she giggled like a bashful librarian. She wasn't sure how she should handle the situation. She didn't know if she should pull her to the side and let her know that the man in her ear was just in her face two days ago or just let Shon do her thing and get in where she fit in.

He must have asked her what she was drinking because Shon responded, pointed to Whitney, and spoke again before he walked toward the bar. At that moment, Whitney decided not to tell Shon anything. If it was meant for her and Chench to connect, then they would. If not, oh well.

When Chench returned with the drinks, he handed one to Shon and the other to Whitney, and they both showed gratitude.

Even though it wasn't evident whether Chench and the girl from campus were an item, judging by Chench's actions, he didn't appear to be too committed. *Bitch probably doesn't know how to keep a man, anyway!* Whitney thought. She was still pissed about the whole incident.

Whitney watched as Chench and Shon danced, but noticed he looked at her more than he should have, considering he had spent the past hour flirting with her friend. As soon as Shon announced that she was going to the bathroom again, he was up in Whitney's face.

"How you doin', beautiful?"

"I'm good." Whitney smiled as she continued to sway to the music.

"You look good, too!"

"Thanks. You don't look so bad yourself."

Chench blushed. "You that chick from the other day, huh?"

"Yup. Where's your crazy girlfriend at?"

"Not here. Can I get you another drink?"

"Sure. Don't forget my girl, too," she added.

He returned at the same time as Shon. Even though they were only three drinks in, she could tell her friend was feeling the effects of the alcohol. It became more evident when she asked if Chench could come back to Whitney's house with them. The inquiry caused a sheepish grin to creep across Whitney's face.

"I'm cool with it," she replied.

Shon spoke into his ear. He looked at Whitney and responded.

Once they finished the drinks he'd just purchased, they exited the club. Shon wanted to leave with Chench, but Whitney blocked it. She also peeped how when he asked for a phone number, Shon told Whitney to give him hers, and Whitney couldn't wait until they got into the car so she could ask her why.

Chapter Fourteen

They had barely made it to the car before Shon began vomiting. Whitney was glad she'd done it outside instead of inside her vehicle, especially since she'd just had her car detailed the week before. She walked over to her and held her hair back until Shon showed signs of improvement. Whitney opened the door and held it until Shon was fully inside. "Put your seatbelt on," she told her and closed the door.

As soon as Whitney got in and buckled up, she looked over at Shon. "Are you okay?"

"Yeah, I'm good. Should have eaten *before* I consumed all that liquor. It's just that I've had little to no appetite since Jackson died. I've already lost close to ten pounds."

Whitney's phone dinged and she unlocked her screen. It was a message from Chench. "He wants to know the address. Do you want me to give it to him?" Whitney held the phone in her left hand and started the ignition with her right.

"Hell, yeah! His ass was cute. Just run me to McDonald's drive-through so I can grab something real quick." Shon lay her head back on the headrest and closed her eyes.

Whitney looked at her in disbelief. “Are you sure? You’re sick and intoxicated, and I don’t need you cheating on your husband tonight and being mad at me in the morning.”

Shon lifted her head and held up her finger. “First, I am *not* sick. My stomach is upset. Second, I ain’t *that* drunk, and I’m *not* married.”

“You’re not? I thought you were.”

“Hell no, I ain’t married—yet.”

“Oh, I thought you and Jackson had a different last name because I called the hospital and gave them the last name Jackson, and they couldn’t find you.”

Shon looked at Whitney and started laughing so hard that she started coughing.

“What’s so funny?” Whitney asked.

“Girl, Ro never told you?”

“Told me what?” Whitney was confused.

“When Ro went away to college, he vowed he was done with the family for good. He dropped our last name, which is Garland, and used his middle name as his last name. So that’s probably why you couldn’t locate me.”

Whitney let out a chuckle, too. “No, he never told me that.” *Damn you, Jackson!*

By the time Whitney and Shon pulled into the driveway, Chench was sitting in his car across the street. When they stepped out, so did he.

"Hey," Whitney called out to him, "give us a few minutes, okay?"

Chench nodded and got back inside his ride. Once they were inside the house, Whitney asked Shon again if she was good. Shon nodded.

"Are you sure about this? Because men don't travel to a woman's house this late at night, under these circumstances, without expecting something in return," Whitney warned her.

"Whitney, I ain't had sex in a minute. My hormones are out of whack, and if I get nothing else tonight, I could really use some head. Shit, that's how I'm guaranteed to get mine, anyway."

"Really?" Whitney asked a bit shocked and surprised. "Me too! That's the only way I can cum! My friends always brag about how good D can make them orgasm multiple times, but that has never been my experience." She felt good, hearing someone else admit it.

"I said 'guaranteed.' I ain't say that's the *only* way," Shon explained.

Whitney swatted at her playfully. "Go get in the shower. I'm going to straighten up a bit and then text him to come in. I'll have him wait in the living room until you're done."

"Bet!" Shon stated and headed toward the spare bedroom.

When Whitney felt the place was presentable, she sent Chench a text, waited until he got to the door, and let him in.

She wasn't sure how the night would play out, but she knew the goal was to have Chench for herself. He was fine and he was the only one who could confirm if that girl was Fredrick's daughter, so there was no way she would hand him over easily. She was just allowing Shon to have her fun and reel Mr. Suave in. Whitney could handle it from there.

"Hey, again." Whitney smiled. "Come on in and make yourself comfortable. Shon should be out in a minute. Can I get you anything?"

"Some water would be nice," he said. "Who shit is this? This a nice little spot."

"It's mine. I just signed the papers a couple of months ago."

"Your man one lucky muhfucka."

"I told you I'm single," Whitney said.

She handed Chench the glass of ice water and watched as he drank the entire thing in what seemed like one gulp. "Thirsty?"

"Nah, just needed to wet my whistle," he answered, while licking his lips.

That made Whitney's vaginal muscles clench. The way he wiggled his tongue gave her the impression he was skilled at using it in other ways. The only thing about being exclusively with white men was that she hadn't experienced any who were great in the oral department. They had no problems performing the act but rarely did she release from it, and the sex was usually hit or miss. The money and perks kept her motivated.

Whitney allowed the comment to linger with no reply. “Sorry, I can’t turn on sports or anything for you. Haven’t hooked my TV up yet.”

“Nah, it’s all good, ma. I’m just here to chill. But if you want me to, I can swing by another time to put that up.”

Boom! Just like that, she had a reason to invite him over again. “That would be great. Otherwise, I’d have to find someone to come do it. You know someone who is good with tools?” It was her turn to be suggestive.

Chench grinned. “Yeah, I know. I’m *very* good with tools!” He reached inside his pocket and pulled out some weed. “Is it okay? You smoke?”

“Nah, that’s not really my thing. But feel free to use the balcony.”

“No problem at all! You do anything besides drink?”

“I have my vices,” she stated.

“Does it happen to look like this?” he asked, producing a small bundle of white powder from a different pocket.

“Now, that’s more like it.”

“Heeyyyy!” Shon sang as she entered the living room, looking refreshed.

Whitney and Chench looked at her and smiled.

“Well, I’ll let you two chat. I’m going to take a shower. Be right back.” Whitney walked off, leaving them to have a little private time. When she returned, she planned to sample Chench's goods in more ways than one.

Chapter Fifteen

When Whitney exited her bathroom, she could hear giggles and kissing sounds coming from the front room. Her portable speaker was playing music and instead of lowering the volume so she could hear them better, she cracked open her bedroom door just a little. Subtle moans permeated the air and traveled into her bedroom. Although she couldn't make out what was being said, she could hear them whisper every now and again. Curiosity was getting the best of her, so she slid on an oversized night shirt and stood at the doorway and listened.

Shon laughed. "Nooo, I am not sucking your dick. I don't even know you like that!"

"Aiight then, so you gonna let me taste that?" Chench asked. "That shit feels so warm and soft. And it smells good, too!'

"Thank you! But slow down, Mr. Go Fast. We've got all night," Shon reminded him. "Maybe after another drink, I'll be in that mood, but right now I'm enjoying your company."

"Bet. Say no more! Wanna smoke?" he offered.

"Nah, no thanks."

"Aiight, well, shorty said I can go out there and blow," he said, pointing toward the sliding glass doors.

"Okay, go ahead. I'll meet you there. Let me grab a sweater or something."

Whitney hurried and acted like she was finishing up as she rubbed more lotion on her arms. Shon tapped on the door.

"Girl, you were right. This dude came to fuck!"

"I told you! You letting him hit?"

"Hell, no! I might let him *lick*."

"What you mean 'might'? Didn't you just say you wanted head?"

"Yes, I did and I do," Shon admitted. "But I can't. As bad as I want to, I don't feel right being with someone else. My dude is a good man. He takes care of home, me, and the kids."

"How'd he get caught up?"

Shon gave a knowing look. "Just like the rest of the 'hood dudes do—drugs. He got a two-to-five. He goes in front of the board in July. We're hoping for parole."

Whitney nodded. She had figured that was it. She couldn't understand why so many inner-city men went that route. There were so many other ways to make money. If they just put a fraction of those hustling skills to use, they would easily excel in other ways legally.

"Hey, it is what it is. Hopefully he comes out and changes his lifestyle. You're a good woman, and those babies need him. I hope you make that clear."

"Oh no, it's been said. No more. If we both have to work two jobs on alternating shifts, that's what we gonna do! I can't do this shit again."

Whitney nodded in agreement. "Well, I'm here for you." As if remembering they had a house guest, Whitney asked where Chench was.

"Oh, he went outside to smoke. Do you have a sweater I can wear?"

"Yeah, look in my closet. Should be one hanging in there."

Shon got up to look. "Girl, do you know he had the nerve to ask me to suck his dick?"

"And?" Whitney asked, perplexed. "That's like intimacy one-o-one. Shit, I was giving head long before I started having sex." Whitney placed the moisturizer on her dresser and searched for her house slippers. "That's my specialty, girl!"

"For real?"

Whitney nodded.

Shon lowered her head for a moment. "You know that has never been my strong point. I mean, don't get me wrong, I've hooked baby daddy up, but I don't think I'm that good, so I don't care to do it."

"Girl, it's easy! Want me to teach you?"

"Seriously? How? I don't want to do it on someone."

"You don't have to. That's what they make cucumbers for." Whitney winked at her.

"Oh, hell yes, B to da FF!"

"I got you," Whitney reassured her. "Now c'mon, let's check on our little friend.

The two ladies headed out to the balcony. Whitney stopped and poured Shon a glass of wine she had in the fridge before stepping out to greet Chench.

"About damn time. I thought y'all forgot about a nigga."

"Of course not." Whitney rubbed his bare arm.

Chench looked down at her hand and then back into her eyes.

"Now, where's 'my kind of party' at?" she asked.

Chench reached inside the small pocket of his pants and handed her the bundle. "That's for you, for your hospitality."

Whitney made brief eye contact with Shon just as she was raising the glass to her lips to take a sip. Shon smirked and winked at Whitney, letting her know that Chench was hers for the taking.

After Whitney consumed her poison and Chench was done with his blunt, they all reentered the condo. Shon had been getting little to no sleep since the baby was born, so she wanted to use the free night to catch up on some Z's. "Look, it's been real. But with a new baby and all, I'm really tired, so I hope you two are okay with me excusing myself."

Chench looked at Whitney. "I'm cool with it."

"Okay, girl. Sleep well. Extra blankets are in the big bag over by the window," Whitney told her. She turned to Chench. "I don't have much, but I do have some wine and Courvoisier.

"I'll take a shot or two of the hard stuff."

Whitney got up and headed to the kitchen. She reached into a half-packed box, pulled out another glass, and washed it out. She poured his drink and handed it to him and then poured some wine for herself. When the slopes were in her system, rarely did she need anything other than wine to elevate her buzz. After she poured her drink, she joined Chench on the couch.

"I can't help it. What was the deal the other day? Is that your girl or not?" Whitney needed answers.

"Yeah and no. I met her the day her daughter turned one. She was having car problems and shit, so I pulled over to help her. We been together for like five years, but it's always some shit. She's one of those independent-ass chicks, who 'don't need a man for shit.' She be buggin' out."

"Maybe her parents taught her well," Whitney suggested.

"Her parents ain't teach her shit! Her moms been locked up since she was a kid and she never met her dad. She just did well for herself and has this attitude that she'll be fine and don't need anybody."

Damn, it's her! Has to be. "Oh, okay." Whitney wanted more information but didn't want to seem too nosy and risk piquing Chench's suspicion. "So, what do you do for a living?" she asked him, changing the subject.

"I'm a mechanic."

Whitney looked at his hands. "Nah, come again. I don't see one callus." She inspected his hands further.

Chench laughed. "Well, damn! You tell me, then."

"If I could tell just based on observation, I would have. Judging by your attire, footwear, and flashy jewels, it can only be one of a few things: You're either in the entertainment industry or the drug game."

Her assessment seemed to catch him off guard. "A drug dealer? Why can't I be a hardworking man, with a legit career?"

"I spend a lot, and I mean *a lot,* of time observing people. I'm really good about sniffing out bullshit and lies."

"I didn't lie."

"You didn't tell the truth, either. I offered two practical suggestions for your livelihood, and you honed in on the drugs. If you weren't in that business, you would have made it blatantly clear. Most people won't allow themselves to be mislabeled, especially not with a title like that."

Chench peeked at her. “What do you do? You a lawyer, or sumthin’?”

“I am, in fact. Right now, I’m working at one of the local LGBTQ centers. See how that works? No smoke screens, no wordplay, no bullshit.” Whitney smiled at her own acuity.

“Yeah, I see. I’m working on some legit things.”

“Such as?”

“I’m trying to open my own boxing gym. It’s a great form of exercise and it teaches self-defense.”

“See, that’s what I like to hear. I shouldn’t be saying this because I’m an officer of the law, but if someone is going to risk their life and freedom doing illegal shit, the least they can do is have a plan to get themselves out of the danger zone. If you’re really serious, I have contacts who can help make that a reality. But first, you have to work on legitimizing your investment capital. Banks are going to want to see W2s and a legal work history.” Whitney adjusted her position on the couch so she was sitting cross legged, facing Chench.

The scent of her lotion overpowered the air he inhaled. The smell instantly turned him on. “True, and I don’t have any of that yet,” he admitted.

Whitney appreciated his honesty. She couldn’t stand a man who always tried to bullshit her. “Well, when you’re ready, let me know. I’ll help you out.”

Whitney looked at Chench, waiting for a response. Chench looked at Whitney with anticipated lust. The only thing he loved more than his mom's pollo con arroz y habichulas was a beautiful woman with a nice brown complexion. Whitney's dark skin and full breasts were exactly what he liked. Couple that beauty with brains, and he had a win-win situation on his hands. Instead of replying, he leaned in for a kiss. Although Whitney didn't reciprocate, she did allow his mouth to caress different parts of her face and neck. When she'd had enough, she slowly moved his head between her legs, lifting her nightdress simultaneously.

Chench wasted no time spreading her legs and placing one of them over his shoulder for easier access. His tongue stroked every crevasse of her vagina before he focused on her clit until she released with gut-wrenching pleasure. Not the one to be outdone, Whitney was sure to return the favor until he came as well.

Whitney was tired and needed some sleep. "It's been a pleasure," she said as she walked to the door, signaling to him that it was time to leave.

"Damn, it's like that?" he asked.

"For right now. But I have your number and you have mine." She opened the door. "Let's not be strangers."

Chench walked to the doorway. "Definitely not," he replied and descended the stairs.

Chapter Sixteen

Whitney had developed a Sunday routine, which entailed reviewing court cases for the upcoming week, calling her dad to catch up, and then meeting Lina and Simone for brunch. This Sunday was different. The orgasm Chench had so generously given her had her sleeping like a hibernated bear. So when she rolled over to continue catching some Z's, she was startled by Shon, who was sitting on her bed, sipping from a Dunkin' Donuts cup.

"What the hell?" Whitney squealed. She adjusted her pillow and sat up a bit. "You scared me! What are you doing in my room?"

"Making sure you didn't slip into a coma," Shon joked. "I called your name a couple of times, and you didn't answer. I wanted to see if you wanted something while I was out. Then when I got back, and I saw you were still sleeping, despite it being a little after noon, I figured I'd wake you."

"Girl!" Whitney started.

"You don't even have to say it. I ain't no creep, or nothin', but I am definitely going to need you to teach me some dick-sucking skills. Yeah, I stayed up to watch. And you swallowed? You know black chicks don't be doing that shit, right?"

"Shon, I *am* black," Whitney reminded her.

"Yeah, by skin color, but you operate like a straight-up suburban white chick, from how you speak, your posture, mannerisms, and style. It's clear ya ass ain't come from the 'hood."

Whitney cut her eyes at her. "I had my fair share of time in the 'hood. I practically lived with my grandparents up past Pine Hills."

"That ain't the 'hood, Whitney. Second and Judson, Lex and First, Elizabeth and Fourth. Now, *that's* the 'hood."

"Are you judging me?" Whitney was growing defensive.

"No, of course not. There's a difference between judging and assessing. I'm stating factual observations, with no opinion. I think you're great. I love your style!" Shon sipped from her cup. "So much so that I *need* you to teach me some moves," she said, borrowing a portion of the line from, *The Last Dragon*, one of her favorite childhood movies. "So when baby daddy gets home, he gonna want to put a ring on it."

Whitney laughed at her antics. "I need food. Let's step out real quick."

She performed a quick hygiene routine and threw on some comfortable clothes. Since it was so late in the afternoon, she opted to go to the local diner for a breakfast sandwich.

"I need to run into Stewart's real quick and grab a scratch off and some rolls to bring back for my mom. Is that okay?" Shon asked.

"Yeah, no problem." Whitney pulled into the lot of the nearest convenience store and waited near the air pump for Shon to return. She turned on the stereo and was changing the CD, when someone banging on the driver's side window startled her.

"You fucking whore! Why, Whitney? Why would you fuck my dad, huh? Of all the people you could have been a slut with, you chose my father?" Patrick was enraged. His bloodshot eyes, disheveled clothing, and the foam in the corners of his mouth proved it.

Whitney looked around, frightened and embarrassed. People were out and about. She exited the car and tried to reason with him. "Patrick, calm down. Let's talk about this."

"The time to talk was months ago. But instead, you blew me the fuck off and, apparently, blew my dad, too. I warned you not to play with my heart."

Whitney was now concerned. His eyes seemed void of a rational soul and his actions were making her feel unsafe.

"What's going on?" Shon asked as she walked back to the car. "You want me to call the cops?"

"No, I—I don't think we need to. Patrick is okay, right? We can go somewhere and discuss this like mature adults, right?" Whitney coaxed.

Shon wasn't a fool. She had read enough and saw enough on TV. She reasoned that an angry white man was the most unpredictable person on earth, and she didn't think Whitney should take his abrupt presence lightly. Her instincts were proven true when Patrick produced a handgun from his jacket pocket. She turned around and ran back into the store to get help.

"Patrick, what are you doing? Please, put the gun away. Look, I'm sorry. I am so sorry about what happened," Whitney pleaded.

"Don't fucking lie to me, you stupid bitch!" he yelled. "You don't care about me."

"I *do* care about you. I really do. That's why I didn't accept your proposal. I knew you deserved better." Whitney was being honest.

"Bullshit! You didn't accept because you like being a goddamned whore."

"That's not true. I really wanted to do right by you. I swear!"

Patrick shook his head and blinked rapidly. He pointed the gun at Whitney and walked closer to her. "Now, you can join my father in hell."

He raised the gun and pulled the trigger, not once but twice. Just as he was going to shoot himself, the police showed up and tackled him to the ground.

Once Shon saw that the police had arrived on the scene, she ran out of the store and went to Whitney's side. "Whitney, are you okay?" Shon cried. "Whitney, answer me, please! Please, let me know you're okay!" Shon was hysterical.

"Ma'am, please step aside." EMT's rushed to Whitney's side as a frantic Shon looked on. "Her vitals are low, but I have a heart rate. We've gotta get her out of here, now," one of the medics reported.

Shon hopped into Whitney's car to follow the ambulance to the hospital. As she pulled out of the parking lot and looked at Patrick, she couldn't help but think that had he been a black man, or any man of color, he would've been dead by now. The reality of his privilege sickened her.

The first person Shon called was her mother to let her know Whitney had a medical emergency and she was at the hospital. Once she got confirmation that Whitney was okay, she assured her she would be there to get her kids. After about three hours, the doctor entered the waiting area and walked over to Shon and Whitney's parents.

"She's going to be okay. One bullet grazed her forearm and the other went clear through her shoulder," the doctor reported.

"Can we see her?" Frederick asked.

"Yes, she just got out of surgery. Once the nurses get her into a room, they will come get you."

"Thank you so much, Doctor!" Bethany said.

Shon clasped her hands in prayer form and placed them over her mouth. "Thank you, Jesus!" she said. She wasn't religious but she believed in God and knew that, thanks to Him, her friend would be okay. Another hour passed before the nurse offered to take them back to see Whitney.

She was still a little dazed from the anesthesia, but Whitney didn't want a pity party, so she did the best she could to convey that. "No tears. I'm alive, right?"

"Girl, you were almost killed!" Shon snapped.

Whitney pointed to the television and Bethany turned up the volume. "That's Patrick's house."

"Police are reporting that, just hours earlier, Jack McNapis was killed by his son for what is being labeled as a crime of passion. Neighbors who witnessed the aftermath are telling us that twenty-four-year-old Patrick McNapis killed his father after discovering he was cheating on his mother. Although authorities have not confirmed this story, we were told that the wife of the deceased is asking for privacy during this difficult time. We will follow up once we have more details," the field reporter stated.

The room grew silent and Bethany and Frederick made eye contact. Whitney noticed the unspoken conversation between them and did her best to refocus.

"Whitney," Bethany began slowly. "What did you do?"

"I don't think this is the right time to badger her, Betty," Frederick intervened.

Shon was feeling uncomfortable, so she kissed her friend on the cheek. "Whitney, I have to get back to the kids. I'll call you later to check on you, okay?"

"Okay. Take my car. I'll get it from you later."

Shon nodded and excused herself from the room.

Once the door closed, Bethany spoke again. "When will be the right time? My child barely talks to me and I rarely see her. In fact, the last time we did grace one another's presence, Mrs. McNapis was running out of my house, frantically looking for 'the whore.'"

Whitney did her best, using all her strength, to raise herself in the hospital bed.

Frederick noticed and tried to calm her down. "Skittles, don't do that. Try to relax, okay?" He had been refereeing his ex-wife and daughter for years, and he could tell by the tension in the room that he would need his white hat again. He looked at Bethany with "please not now" eyes and attempted to comfort his daughter.

Bethany didn't heed his implied warning. "Patrick comes from a good family and has always been a good boy. Evidently, something caused him to snap. Seeing that he allegedly killed his father and attempted to kill you makes me believe that, somehow, you played a part in all this."

Whitney took a long time to speak. She looked from her mother to her father and back to Bethany. "I need you to listen and listen well, Bethany. If I am the cause of any of this, then that means you are the root. I've battled insecurities, complexes, and low self-esteem because of you. You have spent my entire life reminding me of how I'm not good enough, light enough, or talented enough to do anything that would help drive out the negative thoughts that played in my head because of your doing. I wanted to enter the Saratoga Springs Junior Beauty Pageant because my daddy always told me I was the most beautiful girl in the world, but you went right behind him and reminded me that, because of my darker complexion, I was less attractive. My kinky hair needed chemicals so it could be straighter, spending time with my grandparents was ruining me because I was exposed to children who spoke slang, and "ain't" is a word that 'poor people' use.

For as long as I can remember, I was criticized, ostracized, and demonized by my own mother. You made me wear wide brim hats, pants, and long sleeves in the summer, just so my skin wouldn't tan too much. You practically hid me from your friends for as long as you could because you didn't see me as someone they would accept. All this was painfully obvious to me before the age of ten. You have never had my back or supported me and, right now, the best thing you can do is kiss my black ass and get the fuck out of my life forever.

And if I had half the gall as Patrick, you would have been dead a long time ago!"

Whitney gave Bethany the longest, most polarizing glare and turned her back just as her mother left her hospital room in tears.

Frederick stood by, grimacing at the dark truth of his daughter's relationship with her mom. He wasn't sure if he should go after Bethany or stay and comfort his baby girl.

Whitney pushed the button for the nurse. She didn't know if she was feeling the pain of her wounds or the agony of a broken heart, but she needed something to numb both.

"Hi, how can I help you?" an Asian nurse asked.

"I need some more pain meds, please."

The nurse reviewed her chart. "I'm sorry, Ms. Bonesteel. You just had a dose prior to leaving the OR, and you're not due for another until two hours from now." The nurse was polite and delicate. "Is there anything else I can do?" she asked sympathetically.

"No, it's okay," Whitney answered.

She wasn't emotional but having confessed to her mother what she had been holding in for so many years pained her.

The nurse gently rubbed Whitney's good arm and walked out of the room.

"Skittles, was that necessary?" Mr. Bonesteel was nothing short of conflicted. Bethany didn't deserve how

Whitney had just spoken to her, but he also hadn't endured what his daughter had. Even though Whitney had been dodging him for the past couple of months, it didn't stop him from texting her and leaving voicemails, letting her know she was on his mind and how truly sorry he was for having to share the news about having another child. Her anger toward him didn't stop him from boarding a friend's private plane to fly from D.C. to Albany to see about his child.

Whitney never answered him. She lay on her side, wiping away every tear that fell from her eyes. She cried for Patrick, his father, his mother, and herself. She hated that she had been raised by a woman who never found her worthy of so many things and having to admit that out loud produced a level of vulnerability that even she couldn't hide any longer.

"Skittles, please talk to me. Please?" Frederick begged. When he saw that he wasn't going to get her to speak, he slid next to her on the bed and placed her head on his chest. He rubbed and soothed her, holding her tightly as she sniffled and heaved. When she showed signs of regrouping, he got up, grabbed a box of tissue, and handed her a few.

"Daddy, I don't want to talk about Mother, okay?"

He raised his hands in surrender. "Okay, baby, that's fine. We don't have to talk about her. But I do need to know what happened. This is serious, and you are my number one priority, so I have to know what's going on."

Whitney told her dad everything, from the time Patrick called her while she was out with Shon, until the shooting. "It was like he was possessed, Daddy. I've never seen him that way before."

"Well, did you sleep with his father, honey?"

There was no way she was going to admit that, especially to her father. On the few occasions her dad had been in the presence of Patrick's father, he'd always felt the man was overly friendly with his underage daughter and had told Bethany that if he ever got wind of any inappropriate behavior, they'd have to find his body.

"Daddy!" was all she said, but never provided an answer. "After I refused to entertain his idea of marriage, Patrick assumed it was because of someone else, and I guess he thought it was his dad."

Mr. Bonesteel nodded. "That boy has always been a little off to me. He struck me as overzealous and extremely possessive. I warned you about him in the past. I'm just glad *you're* okay. This could have ended much worse. In my line of work, I used to see crazy people like him every day. There was no way they were going to fool me with their words, when their actions told a whole other story."

There was a knock at the door, and in walked the doctor who had performed her surgery. "How are you feeling?" he asked Whitney.

Mr. Bonesteel stood. “Hi, I’m Frederick Bonesteel, Whitney’s father.”

The two men shook hands.

“I’m okay, just in a lot of pain right now,” Whitney said.

“And you will be for a while. You’re a very lucky young lady. Things could have been much worse.” The doctor looked over her chart. “Although there’s not much more we can offer in terms of treatment, you did sustain a significant injury, so I’d like to keep you overnight just to monitor your vitals and maintain wound care.”

“Doctor, I’d really like to go home tonight. I’d much prefer to sleep in my own bed, especially if you all can’t do anything for me here.”

“No, Skittles! He is the professional, and if he feels like you need to be monitored, you will stay.” Her father’s tone let Whitney know the topic was not up for debate. “I’ll stay with you, so you’re not alone.”

The doctor smiled with approval. “Sounds like Dad has spoken. I’ll have the nurse come in and recheck your vitals. If everything looks good, you can resume a light diet, and we’ll get you started with some liquids.” The doctor shook both their hands and exited the room.

Usually, when Whitney faced this much stress, she would inhale a line and feel a lot better. However, that was unlikely since she was being guarded by her dad and isolated from her fix. She would at least feel a little better if she could have access to her electronics.

"Daddy, are you able to go by my house and get my laptop and charger? I want to get caught up on some work and call Lina and Simone to let them know I'm okay."

"I'm not leaving your side. I will call my golf buddy's driver and ask him to go by. What's the address?"

Whitney told him where she lived.

"When did you get this place?"

"Daddy, please, not now."

He held up his hand in submission. Whitney gave her father the information and told him where to find the hidden spare key and her things.

"Sweetie, I don't think you should be worried about work. You should be focused on healing," her father said as he typed the last of his message and looked back up at her.

"That is how I plan to heal. Do you think I should spend time sulking in my own sorrow? Patrick is in a safe place, albeit not a good place. Unfortunately, there's nothing that can be done for his dad; yet, I have over one hundred cases that require my presence this week, and my clients are relying on me to do my job."

"What kind of child have I raised?" her dad asked.

"I'm so glad you asked yourself that because I'm sure your work ethic has rubbed off on me, Mr. 'Prepare for a Trial While Battling the Flu.'"

The two of them made small talk, while Frederick handled business from his handheld device. When he didn't hear a response from his daughter, he looked over at her and saw that she was fast asleep. He carefully placed the blankets over her and kissed her forehead. He knew his daughter was not telling him the whole truth about what happened, but right now that was the least of his concerns. He had to make sure that whatever took place wasn't going to ruin her chances at a successful career, and that meant speaking to the right people. Come hell or high water, there was no way he was letting his child's name be destroyed because of this disaster.

Chapter Seventeen

Whitney stood outside her condo door, waiting for Shon to pick her up. She had called her supervisor at the advocacy center the day before and told them she was hospitalized and she would be there bright and early Tuesday. Whitney used all day Monday to share information about her cases with the other attorney, so she could cover for her. She knew that her colleague wasn't the most organized person, which is why she found it necessary to do so much prep work with her. But that wasn't her only challenge. The doctor had her on driving restrictions for two months, and she was desperately in need of help. She needed someone to take her to work and tote her mobile file cabinet.

Whitney reached out to Shon and was thrilled when her friend agreed to assist her. She offered to pay her a hundred dollars a day for her services. Shon still hadn't secured a job after having to quit when her OBGYN placed her on bed rest during pregnancy so she welcomed the opportunity to make some money off the books. It meant she wouldn't have to report the money to HUD and she could get caught up on bills.

Shon pulled up and got out to get Whitney's things. "I am so sorry I'm late. My car was acting up again and then my mom was late getting to my house to watch the kids. They should be all set for daycare in a week or so, so I won't have this issue again," Shon reassured her.

"Good because I can't stand being late as much as I can't stand a broke, horny man."

Whitney got into the car and did the best she could to buckle herself in. Shon leaned over to help her, and she was grateful.

"Still in a lot of pain?" Shon asked.

"Hell yeah. Seems like it hurts worse today than it did when it happened."

"Sorry that happened to you. Maybe if I had tackled him or something instead of running when I saw the gun, you wouldn't have gotten shot."

"Shon, stop. This is not your fault. You did everything right. Suppose you stayed and you got shot. How would I explain that to your mom? She would have killed me. She looks like she doesn't play any games."

Shon gave her a gracious smile.

Once they arrived at the court house, Whitney told her where to park so they didn't have to pay. When they got inside the courtroom, they reported to the attorney's area. Whitney had Shon unload all the files that were rubber banded together and lay them on the table.

"The stack with the pink sticky note is the violent crimes, the yellow are the fraud cases, and the blue ones are the disorderly conduct cases. Put the yellow on the bottom, then the pink, and then the blue. Organize each bundle according to arrest date and time, with the most recent on the bottom. Then place the bundles as indicated."

"Geesh! Why so bossy?" Shon inquired.

"Not bossy, just in work mode. You'll soon learn that. I'm going to look for my colleague. When you're done, meet me in Courtroom 2 and sit right behind the table on the left."

Shon nodded.

"Oh, and Shon." When they made eye contact, Whitney said, "Thanks so much for your help." She blew her a kiss.

When Shon entered the courtroom, she could tell that Whitney wasn't happy from her expression, coupled with the grin on her opponent's face.

"Your Honor, please just give me another day to sort through the discovery," Whitney pleaded.

"Ms. Bonesteel, we don't have another day to give. Your office has been in possession of the documents for weeks now. Your failure to provide a fair and speedy trial should not fall on the shoulders of the prosecutors."

"I was hospitalized for two days."

"You have colleagues," the judge reminded her. "And unless you have another compelling argument as to why your office was ill prepared today, I have to rule in favor of the prosecution."

"Shit!" Whitney mumbled under her breath.

The judge gave her ruling and was already on to the next case. Lately, Whitney had been wondering if this was the line of work for her. Her track record for representing the LGBTQ community wasn't good. She couldn't seem to exonerate any of her clients. It took her too long to gather discoveries and call motions, and as if that wasn't enough, she couldn't even manage to get favorable pleas for her clients. She spent the next two hours in the courtroom, arguing cases that, deep in her heart, she knew she wasn't passionate about.

During the ride home, Whitney was quiet and although Shon didn't want to interfere with her work, as a friend, she felt obligated to be honest with her.

"Look, Whit. The reason these proceedings aren't working out for you is because you're not giving it your all. You don't seem to be all in."

"Don't you think I know that? I don't need the judgement, okay?"

"That's not what I'm doing." Shon turned left and then took a right, before making the turn onto Whitney's street. "All I'm saying is this might not be the move for you. I know you joined this organization in honor of my brother and to uphold the legal rights of people like him. That's commendable and all, but you gotta do what makes *you* happy and brings you the most joy. You can honor Rohan, love him, and support his cause, but you cannot live for him. It's making you miserable."

"So, what am I supposed to do, just give up on his legacy?" Whitney turned to look at Shon.

"No, of course not. Don't give up on him, just let go of *this* fight. Pursue something else that will bring you fulfillment. Maybe you suck at bringing justice to your clients on this end of the law, but you will make one hell of a prosecutor. That fire to represent this group just doesn't seem to be there, but you are great at cross examining, finding evidence, and proving beyond reasonable doubts. I've seen you in action." Shon touched Whitney's arm. "You've got what it takes, girl. Work your magic from an angle better suited for you."

Shon's words made Whitney confirm what her gut had been telling her. It wasn't that she didn't care about her clients' rights but the passion to represent them in court wasn't there. The truth was she got her ass handed to her in the courtroom and she wanted the satisfaction of winning. If it meant switching sides to find victory, then that's what she planned to do.

Chapter Eighteen

Chench had been reaching out to Whitney since the night he was invited to her house; however, due to her injury and her transition to a new job at the DA's office, she had been lying low. Her intent wasn't to ignore him, but she had a lot going on and didn't want to complicate her life further by fraternizing with Chench.

Her prospective employer had been questioning her about her dealings with Patrick and after weeks of investigating, they finally confirmed that she was not involved in his decision to kill his father. She used that time to evaluate her life and where she wanted it to go. She had been researching new therapists and narrowed down three potential candidates. All were women, but of different ethnicities and Whitney was gravitating toward one over the others. She finished the dishes and went into her room to look for her stash. When she found it, she was offended by its low quantity. She started to call her dealer, but didn't feel like taking the drive to East Mass to see her, so she contacted the next best supplier.

After three rings, her call was answered. "Hi, Chench."

"Oh shit! I thought you forgot about me. Wassup, sexy?"

"No, I didn't ... just had a lot going on, that's all. I was just thinking about you."

"You trying to see me?"

"Actually, I am," Whitney confirmed.

"Good, I'm not too far from you. I'ma come scoop you then I gotta make a run. Wanna roll?"

"Sure."

She quickly brushed her teeth and threw on some jeans and a shirt. Chench sent her a text, letting her know he was outside. Three stops later, they were back at her place. After eating some take out, Whitney excused herself and went to take a shower. Before she could finish, Chench had joined her inside. They washed each other and he inquired about her wound.

"Fuck happened to you?"

"Had an accident. It's practically healed now. The range of motion in my right arm is a little messed up, but other than that, I'm good."

Chench looked at her with pity. "Good. Can't have nothing happening to my baby."

"Your baby?"

"Yeah," he said as he kissed her wound and then her neck."

"Let's get out and into a more comfortable setting."

Whitney turned the water off. She handed a towel to Chench and pulled hers from the rack. Once inside her room, she motioned for him to lie on the bed.

"I missed you," he admitted in between kisses he placed on random parts of her body.

He eventually settled on the sensitive part between her legs. Whitney's uncontrollable moans confirmed that his skills were impeccable. He tickled her love button with his tongue and used his finger to do the same just outside her anus. Whitney's breaths became labored. After spending the first couple of minutes watching him do his thing, she leaned her head back and closed her eyes. Whitney gripped his head with both hands and gyrated into his face. The more intense the feeling became, the more she released, until she was no longer able to resist the impending orgasm.

She returned the oral favor and once they started having sex, she gave Chench the confidence he needed to continue slanging his manhood. He pulled out, turned her around, and sexed her from the back until he announced that he was about to cum. Whitney used her left hand to tickle her clit, and when he started grunting and gripping her tighter, she rubbed faster and came with him.

When Chench pulled out, Whitney got up. "I'll be right back." She returned with a warm washcloth, and instead of handing it to him, she washed him off herself.

Once Chench was all clean, he put his clothes and shoes back on.

"I'm getting kicked out again?"

Whitney laughed. "Not unless you have to get home to your family."

"Nah, I ain't got to be anywhere but here."

"So, your girl just lets you stay out all times of night."

"I told you, me and Shy ain't on it like that. She be trying to control my moves, and I ain't really with that shit. So we stay beefin'. A nigga getting tired of it."

"What does she do for a living?"

"She had a couple of part-time jobs while she was in school, but I guess she just got her license to be some investigator, or some shit. She starting her own business." Chench shrugged and dug into his pockets. He pulled out a small plastic bag.

A smile spread across Whitney's face. "A business, huh? That's admirable. She has a name for it yet?"

Chench spread some of the contents in the fold of a dollar bill and crushed it. Private Eye, or Shy, or some shit like that. I found out about it on a humbug. Bitch ain't even tell me about it." Chench inhaled a line.

"Oh, guess she wanted to surprise you." Whitney indulged too.

"Yeah, she surprised me, alright. But enough about her. What can you tell me about you?" He playfully got on top of Whitney, being careful not to agitate her wound.

She giggled and wrapped her arms around his back.

When Chench was fast asleep, Whitney searched the Internet, looking for more information. Thanks to people oversharing what they do and when they're doing it on social accounts, she was able to locate more details on Frederick's daughter. Although she didn't have an account for herself, she was apparently close to people who did, and they had been doing a diligent job of promoting her business for her. Whitney's brain sparked with an idea right before she, too, closed her eyes and fell asleep next to Chench.

~~~

The sound of chirping birds let her know that the sun had greeted the moon and was ready to take its place. Whitney looked over at the clock on her night stand and was shocked that she had slept well into the morning.

"Chench, wake up. I have to get ready for work. My friend will be here in less than an hour."

Chench rubbed his eyes. He, too, surprised by the time. "Shit, I was supposed to hit the road with my mans. You got an extra toothbrush?" He slid his jeans on and then his sneakers before walking into the bathroom.
~~~

"Check the second drawer," Whitney said from the shower. "The tooth paste is in the medicine cabinet."

By the time Whitney got out, she heard Chench telling the person on the other end of the phone that he would see them soon.

"And don't bring that new nigga with y'all. You and Dollar be doing too much. I don't know him and don't trust him." He ended the call and turned to Whitney. "Listen, I gotta bounce, but I wanna see you later on. Is that okay?"

"Sounds good to me."

She let Chench out and quickly finished getting dressed. By the time she was done fixing her hair, Shon was blowing the horn.

Whitney got into the car and immediately started spilling what had been on her mind. "I don't think I ever told you about Mitch, the man who beat up my aunt Valene and attacked my Pa, did I?"

"No, I don't think you did," Shon said, confused about the random topic.

"Well, my aunt was dating this crazy man named Mitch, who had become obsessed with her. He showed up at the school library and began verbally abusing her and being physical because she was studying with her male classmate. She decided that was the last straw and ended the relationship. One evening, he came to Nana and Pa's house, looking for my aunt. Of course Pa wasn't going to let him in, knowing what he had done, so he told him she wasn't there. This sick jerk ended up punching my Pa and pushed him to the floor. He went through the house, calling out to my aunt Valene. Nana picked up the phone to call nine-one-one, and he slapped it out of her hand. Well, I went to pick it up and finish what Nana had started, but he took the phone from my hand, twisted my arm, pushed me on the floor, and left."

"Get outta here! How long ago was this?" Shon asked.

"I had to be about eleven, so about thirteen years ago. I never forgot that night and always said I was going to get revenge on him."

"What do you have in that head of yours? He's probably still crazy, girl. Don't go poking a beast."

"I'm not. I have something else in mind."

"Like what," Shon asked skeptically."

"I told you the first time I met Chench was when I went to the school, hoping to encounter my father's daughter, but that turned bad."

"Yeah, I remember that and you two recognized each other that night at the club," Shon added.

"Right, well we've been getting together, and he recently told me my father's daughter has a private investigator business. Before all of this sibling business, I was in the car with my father when my aunt Valene called. She was on speaker phone telling my dad that she'd gotten word that Mitch was asking about her, and she said 'he better keep his married, psychotic ass away from me.' I think I'm going to act like his wife and have him investigated by my so-called sister's private eye company."

"Are you serious, Whit?"

"Yes, I am very serious. I hate Mitch's guts, and if I can dig up some dirt on him and send it to his wife, she'll probably leave him."

"I'm sure she will, but if he's that crazy, do you think he's going to let her go that easy?"

"I don't know. That's his problem, not mine." Whitney opened the car door and stepped out. "I'll be sure to keep you posted, though." Whitney grinned, thinking about the witty plan she had concocted.

Chapter Nineteen

Whitney sat across from both her parents, unsure of who she wanted to lash out at first, Bethany, because of her disdain for the woman who birthed her, or Frederick, for having them in the same room. When her mother had texted her, and her father called telling her to be at Bethany's house because it was a "family emergency," she thought it had to do with her grandparents. Now, as she sat in front of them to discuss her situation with Patrick, she wished she had never accepted the invitation. Frederick was adamant about Bethany and Whitney at least being respectful to one another, getting to the bottom of the situation with Patrick, and convincing Whitney to forgive him for not telling her about her sister sooner. It was obvious to him she still held the grudge.

"I already told you, what Patrick did has nothing to do with me!" Whitney leaned forward in her seat. "The detectives already investigated and deemed me clear of any wrongdoing. Furthermore, if his stuffy cunt for a mother wasn't so—"

Bethany gasped. "Whitney, do not use that language in my house." She looked at Frederick. "See what I mean? She is completely out of control and has no respect for anyone."

"No, Mother, I just don't have respect for you!" Whitney shot back.

"Skittles, please! Okay. I didn't come here to listen to you berate your mother, and I most certainly didn't call this meeting to serve as referee. My main concern is to make sure you are not culpable for any of that boy's conduct in any way, shape, or form. Just because you were cleared legally doesn't mean they can't come after you in other ways. Now, I know you said you had nothing to do with his actions, but what exactly would cause him to track you down with a loaded gun to try and kill you?"

"I already told you, your daughter was sleeping with his father," Bethany reminded him.

"Is that true?" Frederick asked Whitney for the second time. His eyes revealed that he knew the truth, but his expression begged her to tell him otherwise.

Whitney contemplated lying to her dad. She didn't want to do anything that would ruin his image of her. Yeah, he knew about her hypersexual activity in school and had even tried to convince Bethany that it was typical teenage hormones. But this ... This was a whole other dynamic to her sexual misconduct and although she didn't want to admit it to her father, she knew she had to.

"Yes, it's true, Daddy." Whitney lowered her head in shame.

Frederick cussed and paced. He rubbed his chin and neck, the same way Whitney did when she was anxious. “Did he force you?” Frederick was determined to divert the blame from his daughter, but when Whitney answered, she further crushed his hopes.

“No, he didn’t make me.” She looked up at her father. She saw his demeanor shift from understanding to upset, and it caused her defenses to kick in. “What, does that ruin your image of me? Huh, Daddy? Does that make you wish you’d had another child, a more normal one, with less embarrassing baggage? Oh wait, you *do* have another child. Because just like me, you can’t keep your privates to yourself.”

“Watch your mouth, girl,” Frederick warned. He gave her a stern look.

“Oh, I watch my mouth, Daddy. I am very careful about where I place it. Do I disgust you?” Whitney walked closer to her father. “Are you afraid that you created the female mini-version of yourself? Well, you did! Yeah, I may have slept with Patrick’s dad, did things to and for him that were immoral, but how could I know otherwise when I wasn’t taught otherwise?”

Whitney looked at her mother, who was off to the side with her hand to her mouth, looking like she wished she could blink this whole thing away.

“There’s been times when I was supposed to be spending time with you and you left me in the car while you ran inside ‘real quick,’ only for you to come out, adjusting your belt buckle. Or the times when we stayed at the indoor waterpark or other vacation hotels and after you thought I was asleep, you allowed a mom—who we'd just seen downstairs—to come into the room, and y'all would enter the bathroom and close the door."

"Whitney, enough!" Frederick walked away from her and stood on the other side of the coffee table.

"Enough, because you don't want me to recount any more of your man-whore ways or enough because you don't want Mother to hear it? Well, if it's the latter, then don't you worry, Daddy, Bethany is a known slut, too."

Whack! Bethany had walked over to Whitney and slapped her across her cheek. She stood back with a mixture of horror and regret etched into her face.

Whitney rubbed the side of her face. She looked back and forth between her parents. She walked to the kitchen and retrieved her purse from the barstool.

"If you ever put your hands on me again, it will be your very last time breathing." She gave her mother the look of death. She walked over to her father. "Fuck you! And fuck that bastard-ass child of yours."

Whitney pulled open the front door so hard that it crashed against the foyer wall. She left, vowing to never speak to either of her parents again. As soon as she got to her car, she called Chench to see if he was available. She wanted to release some steam but didn't want to go home. He told her to meet him in the parking lot of his friend's apartment. After getting the address she headed in that direction. When she arrived, she got into his car and he drove off.

"I gotta run in the store real quick and get me a blunt. Want anything?"

"Just a water for now, please." She scanned her surroundings and immediately locked the doors when he got out.

Whitney sat in the passenger seat, going through his glove compartment and arm rest, when she came across a business card for Private EyE, with a number and email address. *What is he doing with her business card if they broke up?* Whitney wondered.

Her thoughts were cut short by the two women who had appeared on either side of Chench's car. One was trying to grasp her door handle, while the other did the same on the driver's side.

"Get the fuck out the car, bitch!" one girl yelled.

"You fucking with my friend's man?! We gonna beat ya ass!" the other screamed.

Whitney looked on in confusion. She had never seen the two girls a day in her life, but they seemed convinced that she was their intended target. She was glad she'd had enough sense to lock the doors and felt safe talking back.

"Y'all are crazy! Get the hell away from this car," Whitney yelled. They were both now standing on her side. "Screw you, too! I don't even know y'all!"

Whitney looked up and saw Shy walking out the store, with Chench not too far behind her.

"Get out the car then, bitch," one of the girls said.

"Yeah, since you got so much shit to pop on the inside, you punk ass," the other one yelled.

"Shakyra, Chanel, let's go. It's cool," Shy said. "Ain't no need to rag her.

She seemed more reasonable and rational this time around.

"You lucky," the shorter of the two girls stated before she kicked the passenger side door for good measure. They were clearly drunk. The taller girl slurred a lot of her words.

"What the fuck y'all doing?! Don't be tearing up my shit!" Chench yelled.

Once he got inside the car and pulled off, Whitney questioned him. "Who was that, and what was that about?"

"Shy and her crazy-ass friends."

"Are you still with her?"

"Hell no! Them bitches just drunk and starting shit. She asked me if I was coming to her place tonight and I told her no. I'm not fucking with her like that."

Whitney hoped he was telling the truth because she wasn't sure if she could handle any more violent encounters. Fighting wasn't her thing, but clearly, Shy and her friends lived by a different code, one of which Whitney wanted no parts.

Chapter Twenty

The switch to the DA's office was the professional change Whitney needed. After only a few weeks on the job, she immediately knew it was a better fit for her. She had gotten most of her cases to plea and had won the few that did go to trial. Even though Whitney's doctor had lifted her restrictions, she had decided that Shon was an asset and asked if she would be willing to stay on as her assistant, and Shon agreed. Today, she had a pretrial hearing scheduled and, although she had arrived early, her assistant was late. To kill time, she chatted with one of the senior prosecutors hoping Shon would be there soon. Whitney looked at her watch and determined that she couldn't continue to wait. She fared her colleague well and turned to walk inside the building.

"Wait, Whit, I'm right here!"

Whitney turned to see Shon exiting a cab and walking briskly to her side. "I know you don't want to hear any excuses, but I swear it wasn't me. My damn car wouldn't start again, so I had to walk the kids to daycare and then wait for a cab to get me. He had like two other stops before mine."

"You *do* know you always have an excuse, even though that's not what you call them."

"They're reasons, not excuses," Shon said, correcting her.

"Whatever. You're still late. I don't understand why you don't get rid of that piece of junk," Whitney countered. She smiled at the security guard and waited for Shon to retrieve her badge from her bag before they were allowed through.

"Well, not everybody makes five grand a month, tax free, just for fucking," Shon shot back.

Whitney gave her a look.

"I'm sorry. That was wrong of me. I shouldn't have—"

Whitney held up her hand. The words had already been said. She didn't want to hear her friend's awkward attempt to smooth them over. "Did you finish that motion I emailed you last week?"

"Yes, I even scanned it and sent an electronic copy to your work email and had the certified copies delivered to the judge and the defense attorney a few days ago."

Whitney complimented Shon with a grin.

"Counselor, you're late!" Judge Brandon barked as soon as Whitney stepped inside.

"I accept full responsibility for my tardiness, Your Honor." Whitney laid her file on the table and pulled out the relevant documents.

The judge slipped on his glasses. "Let's proceed."

"Your Honor, we have a motion to suppress the testimony of the defendant's, nurse, Margaret Wilkes."

"Under what grounds?" Walter Benson, the defense attorney, asked.

"Did you not receive Ms. Bonesteel's motion prior to this pretrial hearing?" Judge Brandon inquired.

Whitney and the rest of the gallery watched as Benson looked through his files and briefcase. "Your Honor, I was never sent any motion."

"False!" Whitney retrieved the signed confirmation and read it aloud. "On Thursday, May 22nd at 3:06 p.m., someone in your office signed for it."

"Let me see that." Benson took the paper from Whitney's hands and dropped his head after making out the signature. "This was my secretary, and she must have forgotten to give it to me before she left for vacation. I would like to request a continuance until I've had a chance to review it, Your Honor."

"That's not going to happen, Counselor. Ms. Bonesteel did her due diligence and, although it's unfortunate for your client that you weren't able to prepare, I cannot delay the proceedings any further." Judge Brandon looked at Whitney. "Counselor, you may have the floor."

"Your Honor, I entered a motion to suppress the testimony of the doctor's nurse who—as a reminder to the court and the unprepared defense attorney—"

"Your Honor!" Benson cried.

"Counselor, we will not be offensive to the members of this court," Brandon chided.

"Understood. As I was stating, Margaret Wilkes's testimony is biased."

"On what grounds?" Benson intercepted.

"If you give me a chance to *swallow* and finish my sentence, you'll see," Whitney rebutted.

Benson's face flushed.

"There's evidence that she and the defendant had been having an affair; therefore, the key witness in this case is compromised."

"Objection! My client's nurse has been a dedicated employee of his for two decades, which has extended their familiarity in ways that may warrant more casual engagements but none of a sexual nature."

"Counselor, what evidence are you presenting to support your motion to dismiss this witness," Judge Brandon questioned.

"I'm glad you asked, Your Honor. When I think of extended familiarity, barbeques, double dates, kids' school plays, and other platonic social engagements come to mind, not intimate dinners and hotel rendezvous." Whitney handed Brandon and Benson a photo of Benson's defendant and his nurse inside a restaurant, holding hands, another photo of them kissing, one of them entering a hotel together, and one more showing them making out inside the hotel room, all compliments of a private investigator's work. She even had copies of the receipts to corroborate the photos, which was her own doing.

Benson lowered himself into the seat next to his client. He leaned his elbow on the table and used his thumb to massage his temple. Whitney turned and grinned at Shon and briefly turned to face the courtroom.

Judge Brandon said, "Well, this is condemning evidence to support the prosecutor's motion. Do you have anything to say, Counselor?" Brandon looked at Benson, who was still conversing with his client. "Counselor!" he called again.

"Your Honor, we would like to accept the prosecutor's plea deal and avoid trial."

Whitney walked out of the courtroom, smiling wider than an actor in a Colgate commercial. She was hugging Shon and celebrating her victory, when Benson approached them.

"Well, congratulations. I honestly didn't think you had it in you to perform so well—at least in these kinds of rooms," he jeered.

Whitney snickered. "That's an acceptable comment, coming from a man with such a small head." She looked down at his crotch and then back at him. "Just know that Whitney Bonesteel performs well in any setting, especially *rooms*." She winked at him. "Maybe next time, Counselor … or not!"

When Benson walked away with his tail tucked between his legs, Shon and Whitney laughed long and hard.

"Yo, what the fuck was that about?" Shon prodded.

"Oh, he was a sponsor I'd serviced a couple of times before. Met him while working at the LGBTQ agency. It was literally only twice. He had this swallowing fetish, and I refused the first time. He offered me triple the second time we met up, and I almost obliged."

"So, what happened?" Shon pressed.

"He tried shoving his cock further into my mouth while holding my head in a death grip. But that didn't bother me. When he said 'drink my cum, you black, sexy bitch,' he fucked up. Nobody calls me out of my name." Whitney laughed and Shon laughed with her.

"I tell you, you amaze me more and more each day. I'm gonna start calling you 'Bones.' If your skeletons are anything like your body count, I'ma have to name a cemetery after your ass."

Whitney cocked her head to the side. "You know what, that doesn't sound like a bad business idea!"

Whitney was always looking for more ways to increase her revenue. A cemetery would be the perfect investment and thought of her plan. She was going to need a place to bury Mitch's bones and figured a cemetery named after her family would be a fitting place.

Chapter Twenty-One

Whitney held the phone to her ear and used her shoulder to hold it in place; she removed items from her fridge to make a sandwich, and waited anxiously for Shon to answer the phone. Whitney had called Shon back to back, and the first call went unanswered. She was so excited about the success she was experiencing in her new role that she wanted to share it with her friend. She was about to leave a message when Shon answered on what was probably the last ring.

"Hey, girl!" Shon sounded exhausted.

"Hey, back at you. Are you okay? You sound like crap," Whitney admitted as she cut a tomato.

"Geesh! Thanks, friend!" Shon said.

"I'm just being honest. Isn't that what friends do? Anyway, what's going on?"

"Too much! Quazier didn't sleep at all last night. He was cranky and whined for hours. Quayvianna woke up with a fever yesterday morning and had diarrhea and has been throwing up since. As if that wasn't enough, their dad called me fussing about not receiving a visit or a package and telling me I ain't holding him down like I promised. It's like I'm only one person. I'm doing the best I can to keep up with the bills, get my car fixed, keep food in the house ..." Shon's voice trailed off. Her silence was telling.

Her subtle sobs confirmed to Whitney that life was getting the best of her, and it stirred emotions inside Whitney that she didn't know she had. All her life, Whitney had gone about living for herself. She never cared about what others were going through, because it wasn't her business. Her primary focus had always been Whitney and until now, she had no reason to change that. As she witnessed her friend's struggles, it compelled her to act in a way she never had—unselfishly.

"Is there anything I can do?" Whitney asked. Although it felt weird to offer something to someone, saying it made her feel good.

Shon laughed a bit. "I think that's the first time you've offered to help me with something instead of offering to pay me to help you with something."

Whitney smiled. "I guess you can say I get it honestly. My dad always said there's nothing free in this world and everything comes at a cost. Sometimes, we don't always find out what that cost is until later. Let's just say I'm not a fan of surprises."

"The fact that you offered means a lot."

"I'm serious. What can I do? I know you haven't accepted my offer to vacation with me in sixty days, but it still stands. Plus, you sound like you could use a getaway."

"Girl, as good as that sounds, I don't think I'll be able to go. My mom didn't seem too keen on the idea of watching the kids for a week while I'm off on a beach, sipping pretty drinks with fruit and umbrellas in 'em. Plus, I can't afford that shit right now. I need a new car, my fricking utility bill is past due, and I need to be looking for a full-time job now that my maternity leave is over."

Whitney placed the sandwich ingredients on the bread, poured on her homemade dressing, sprinkled salt and pepper, and put the sandwich together. She heard her phone beep and looked at the caller ID.

"I hear you. Listen, that's Chench. Can I call you right back?"

An exasperated Shon replied, "Sure."

Their call ended.

"Hey, what's up?"

"You," Chench replied. "I wanna see you. Can I come through?"

Whitney looked around at her place and reasoned that it was just too messy to try and clean before he got there. She had just bought more stuff for the condo and the bags were still strewn about. She had a bunch of laundry to do and she desperately needed to sweep and mop.

"Uh, my place is in disarray right now. Can we go to your spot?"

Chench thought for a second. "Well, I'm kind of in between places right now, but I just helped my man and his family move, so we can camp out at his shit for the night."

"Sounds good to me. Text me the address."

It didn't take long for the information to come through. Whitney showered, got dressed, and headed to meet Chench. When she arrived, he was standing outside his car, waiting on her. Whitney followed Chench inside the small apartment, and instead of decorated walls, furniture, and carpeted floors, she was greeted by a hallow room. A couple of boxes sat on the floor not too far from where a laundry hamper, a fan, and a few bags were neatly placed. She turned in all directions and caught sight of a 10x13 photo of what appeared to be a young woman and a small child. She looked up at Chench, and he was looking at her.

"Hear me?" he asked a zoned-out Whitney. "I said my man gonna come get that stuff tomorrow. I figured we could make a little pallet on the floor."

Whitney looked at him and around the room. "Sure. No problem." She walked closer to him and gently grabbed his neck. "How about you go make the pallet, then?" She needed him out of the room so she could do her own investigating. Her instincts were telling her Chench wasn't being truthful.

Chench leaned in and kissed Whitney on the mouth. He was hoping she'd part her lips for him, but it didn't happen. "Sexy ass!" He slapped her thigh and walked to the back of the house.

Whitney perused the room and stepped closer to get a better look at the photo. Just as she'd suspected, this wasn't his "man's" apartment. The photo was a picture of Shy and her daughter. *This must've been her place, and if she moved, where did she go?* There was a piece of mail poking out from one of the bags, so Whitney leaned down to get a closer look. "Chaianne Lewis." *Chaianne. Chai, not Shy!*

"All set! Chench reappeared. "Whatchu doin'?" He walked toward her.

Whitney touched a spot on the carpet and rubbed her pointer finger and thumb together as she stood up straight. She brought those same fingers to her nose. "Were these carpets cleaned? It smells damp in here," she said, pretending to observe something that Chench had missed.

"Nah, not that I know of, but c'mon ... I got us all set up." He walked over to the picture and tried to turn it around, not knowing Whitney had already seen it.

Whitney and Chench were in the back room, engaging in their usual antics, when a noise caught her attention.

"Did you hear that?"

"Hear what?" Chench asked in between licks.

"I think I heard something out there. Go check."

"It's probably the neighbors coming in. I told you my boy won't be back until tomorrow. Relax, and let me do that shit you like."

Whitney ignored her gut and continued enjoying the feeling Chench was giving her. He was nuzzling her neck in a manner that caused her to release moans and giggles. Those feelings were interrupted when the door opened abruptly and the lights flicked on.

"Oh, now you done fucked up!"

Chaianne looked visibly pissed and rightfully so. If the incident at her school was any indication of what she was capable of, Whitney wanted no parts. When Chench jumped to his feet in search of his boxers, Whitney hopped up to brace herself for what was to come.

"Bitch, didn't I tell you not to fuck with me?" Chaianne said as she charged towards Whitney with raised fists. Every blow connected with each word she spoke.

"Get her off me!" Whitney yelled to Chench.

He was on the other side of the room, trying to get his boxers on before coming to her rescue.

Whitney held her head down as Chaianne continued to uppercut her in the face. Chench tried to intervene to help Whitney, but Chaianne pushed her in another direction and turned her wrath toward him. Whitney watched helplessly as Chaianne threw punches and kicks at him, trying her best to inflict damage.

"You grimy muthafucka!" she yelled. "You bring the next bitch into my house?!"

"Chill the fuck out! I didn't know you was still staying here," Chench said as he grabbed her by the wrists and held her against the wall.

"What do you mean you didn't know I was still staying here? Nigga, this is my shit! Did you forget?"

"When I came by yesterday and saw most of your things were gone, I assumed you left me."

"And you assumed right. But you still thought it was cool to bring a bitch to an apartment you shared with me? Huh, Dom? I can't believe this. You know what, get your fucking hands off me," Chaianne spat.

Chench released her arms, and she shoved him. He was sure to stand between Chaianne and Whitney as Whitney stood against the wall, covering herself with a blanket.

"Bitch, if I didn't have so much going for myself, I would use your ugly ass to shine these floors. You the type of chick that deserves to get stomped the fuck out. But you know what? Your day is coming. This, I promise you, Jasmine."

Chaianne walked out of the room and left the house, slamming the door behind her. Whitney was relieved it was over and started to get dressed.

"Damn, where you going? It ain't like she comin' back!" Chench pleaded.

"I don't care if she does or doesn't. I just know I won't be here to find out." Whitney grabbed the last of her clothing and put them on. "Are you staying here or coming with me?"

Chench looked at her pleasingly. "I didn't think you were gonna ask." He grabbed his stuff and as if just realizing what Chaianne said, he turned to Whitney, "Yo, why she called you Jasmine?"

"Oh, I used to mess with a guy who went to her school and that's what I told him my name was." Whitney half lied. She did go by the name Jasmine, she just left out the part of having been with multiple guys at that school and using that as her alias. She walked past him and straight to her car before he had a chance to ask any more questions.

Even though Chaianne may have physically gotten the best of Whitney, on more than one occasion, there was no way she would win the war. In Whitney's mind, she had been violated one too many times and as a mental fighter, all she needed was a day or two to plot revenge on a person she'd never even liked in the first place.

Chapter Twenty-Two

Feeling bad about abruptly ending the call with Shon to accept Chench's, Whitney woke up the next day, placing several calls to her friend. After her multiple attempts were unsuccessful, Whitney decided to focus her efforts on Chaianne. The campus fight, the attack by her friends, and the assault from the night before, confirmed that Whitney had no choice but to hit Chaianne where it hurts—in the pockets. She knew she couldn't beat her physically, but based on her conversations with Chench, she knew just how much Chaianne's new business meant to her. If she could destroy the business, she knew she could weaken the volatile beast and leave her just as broken as when she was abandoned by her mother.

Whitney was glad she had taken a picture of Chaianne's business card when she'd found it in Chench's car because now, it came in handy. She dialed the number on the card and after several rings, was greeted by a voicemail. "Hi. You've reached Private EyE, your personal resource for your private affairs. I'm unable to take your call at the moment, but please leave your name, number, and a brief message, and I'll get back to you at my earliest convenience. If you'd like, feel free to email me at privateeye@info.com. Have a blessed day."

Whitney opted to forego the voicemail and instead, opened her internet browser and sent a message to the provided email address:

Hello, my name is Tara Robinson, and I believe my husband of fifteen years has been having an affair. I am interested in hiring you to obtain proof. Please email me back with availability. Thank you.

As soon as Whitney hit send, she looked up and saw Chench walk through the door carrying bags. "Hope you're hungry! I stopped and got us some takeout." He placed the bags on the counter. "What you was doin'?"

"Oh, nothing, work stuff." Whitney closed her laptop.

"Here." He handed her a bag with a box in it. "I saw these and thought they'd look nice on you."

Whitney opened the bag and box and grinned. "I love them, Chench. Thank you!" The cage-style open-toe wedges would complement a lot of her attire. She secretly wondered how he'd gotten her size since he'd never asked. *Probably looked at a pair of my shoes,* she reasoned.

Whitney watched as Chench walked over to the sink to wash his hands, then return to the table.

"Why you looking at me like that?" he asked.

"Can I ask you a question? And I need an honest answer, too." Whitney started pulling dishes from the cabinet so she could plate the food.

"What's up?"

"Are you and Chai still sleeping around? I mean no one acts like this over a man she is no longer with. She physically assaulted me twice, and I'm in the right mind to press charges," Whitney lied.

Chench walked over to her. "Charges? Hell no! Don't do that shit. She has a kid and it won't be fair to her daughter if her mom has to go away and do time. Leave that shit alone. We ain't involving the law in this. I'll teach you how to fight," Chench joked, avoiding Whitney's question.

"You play too much. Seriously, are you still with her?"

"Nah, we're done. I told you that. "

"Well, when's the last time *you* saw her?" Whitney asked.

"Not since that night. Why you asking me all this?"

"I just want to make sure you're not playing both sides. There's a lot of things I'm willing to share, but you aren't one of them."

"You ain't got to worry about that. I'm all yours, baby."

Whitney grinned inwardly. "So listen, have you given more thought to going legit?"

"Actually, I have. This hustling shit is starting to get draining."

"Good, because it's also getting old. The cops are cracking down on street dealers and I can't have you getting locked up on me. Plus, I have an idea. I think we should form a venture capital business and use our money to invest in other small businesses." *Like the one your crazy ex started.*

"How we gonna do that? Honestly, I'm a little skeptical about how all this is gonna work. You sure we ain't doing nothing illegal? I'll chance the 'hood shit, but once you start fucking with the 3-letter boys, that's when those prison numbers get real."

Whitney walked toward him and stroked the side of his face. "Do I look like the prison type? Of course it's legit, if it was illegal I wouldn't be doing it. This is what I have in mind: Together, you and I will create MoneyWorx. MoneyWorx will loan small sums of money, as low as $1000, but no more than $10,000, to small businesses looking to either get off the ground or expand. Not all businesses have the credentials to obtain a bank loan or other resources to turn their dreams into reality, and that's where we come in. We will pool together our funds and make our money work for us by loaning to startup businesses, and they'll pay us back with interest. Simple as that."

"And how do we know these businesses will thrive? I mean what if they flop? Then what?"

Whitney smiled and grabbed Chench's hand. "That's a risk we take, but we would have already done the necessary checks and balances to ensure that the business is, and will be, operating in the black by reviewing their product, market size, potential problems, solutions, competition, traction, and current earnings. If the potential is there, we'll go for it. If not, we won't. I've already done my research, and based on the fifty or so business I've looked into, I have a startup company in mind that will work."

"And what company is that?"

"It's a new, shall we say, surveillance company. Our society is becoming more and more obsessed with being in the know and with the right investors, I'm confident this particular company will be very successful," Whitney explained, placing kisses around his face.

Chench palmed her backside with both hands and pulled her into him. "You so fucking smart, beautiful, and sexy." He said before going straight for her lips. Whitney slightly turned her head. Chench looked into her eyes. "I'ma make you my wife one day, you know that…you love me?"

"No, I didn't know that. And I'm not sure if that's the way love goes. Wouldn't we both have to be in agreement? Can't we just be with each other without emotional obligations and contractual attachments?" The topic stressed Whitney out.

"Damn! You just can't let me penetrate that emotional muscle, can you? This is how love goes: When two people care for each other, they usually develop feelings, exchange terms of endearment, and make plans for the future. You actin' like you ain't neva been in love before."

Whitney thought for a moment, "Can't say that I have." The hard truth was she didn't know what that entailed.

The ringing house phone was a welcome distraction to the deep talk she didn't feel like having so she answered it immediately. "Hey, girl. What you doing?"

"I was in the shower and heard my phone ringing like crazy. That was you calling back to back?" Shon replied.

"Yeah. I wanted to stop by real quick. Is that okay?"

"Yes, that's fine."

"Okay, Chench just got in with some food. As soon as we're done, I'm going to stop by. I'll text you when we're close."

When Whitney shared with Chench that she wanted a new car, he'd wasted no time introducing her to his go-to salesman and after a week of searching he had helped her find the vehicle she was looking for. Her only requirements was that it was a red car, with leather interior and it had to be a convertible and to her delight, that's exactly what he found. Now, she was ready to pass along her old car to someone who could really use it and was looking forward to gifting it to someone who could really use it.

~~~
~~~

When she pulled up in front of Shon's house, she blew the horn several times before exiting. By the time she made it to the curb, Shon was at the front door.

"What in the ..." Shon said when she saw Whitney carrying a bouquet of balloons and a letter.

"I just wanted to do something nice for you. I see you out here being Superwoman, trying to maintain your sanity, along with everything else, and I thought you deserved a little pat on the back."

Whitney handed Shon the balloons and envelope. After they hugged, Whitney told her to open it. Inside was a bundle of one-hundred-dollar bills, a set of keys, and a note. Shon read it and burst into tears. "You didn't have to do this, Whitney. Your loyalty and devotion are enough. I don't even know what to say. Like ... thank you so much."

"You deserve it. This is the bonus you earned. You are a great employee and your thoroughness has helped me win quite a few cases."

Shon placed her hands on her eyes as tears continued to fall on her face. "How are you gonna get to work? Does this mean I have to be your driver still too?"

"Nooo, I have something in the works. Plus, Chench can chauffer me until my car is ready, it should only be a few days. This car is paid off, it's reliable and I just figured I'd give it to you than trade it in. Plus, it originally was a gift from my parents so I wanted to treat myself to a distraction from them."

"Wow, so you two are hitting it off kinda tough I see," Shon looked towards Chench's car. "You fallin' in love, Bones?"

"Heck no, you know Bones doesn't fall in love, baby." They laughed. "But I do like him a lot. I've never had anyone like him. He seems genuinely into me, surprises me with things, has amazing head and dick skills, it's like he's my total package. Not white, not black, but the best of both worlds. I really like him."

"Good for you! I was starting to wonder if you'd ever turn in your hoe passport! You're the only twenty-four-year-old I know who's had sex in more places than local bitches have seen on TV."

Whitney bent over laughing. "Shush, not too loud! He might hear you." She said as she turned in his direction. "Listen, I have to go. Enjoy everything because you deserve it. I can't wait until we hit the sky in a few weeks." Whitney hugged Shon and descended the stairs.

"Sky? Girl, I told you I can't go anywhere!" Shon placed her hand on her hip.

"I know what you said. Now, let me do what I do with it." Whitney winked and got into Chench's car. From the sideview mirror, she could see Shon walk over to her new 5 Series BMW sedan. Her friend's excitement was the last thing she witnessed before they turned the corner.

Chapter Twenty-Three

The courtroom was abuzz, the city of Albany had just arrested twenty people in a planned sweep of one of the most notorious drug rings; and there were more people showing up to support the defendants than the court could hold. Whitney immediately thought of Chench and once she looked over the entire list of arrestees, she sighed in relief, glad that her dude wasn't one of them. The amount of people moving about the small courthouse was beginning to overwhelm her. Her cases kept getting moved to different courtrooms and now she was having a hard time locating where she was supposed to report next.

"Whit!" Shon called out to her. When she got Whitney's attention, she waved her over. "I called you like three times, girl. C'mon, your case has been moved to courtroom C."

Whitney and Shon entered a full room, but at least they weren't sitting on top of each other like they had been in the other two rooms. The judge called her first case, which resulted in a plea, as did the next three. It was pretty easy to get the defendants to agree when there was blatant evidence of their guilt. Plus, she'd gone a little easier on them since they were older, first-time offenders. Whitney tried hard to focus on the rest of the cases, so much so that she hadn't noticed Shon sitting behind her in a disturbed trance. She quickly gathered her things so she could see about her friend, when she noticed how enthralled Shon was with the next docket.

"The People versus Gordan Stellman," the judge announced.

Once the defendant and his attorney stood at the bench, the judge continued. "Mr. Stellman, you are being charged with murder in the second degree. Between the times of eight-thirty p.m. and nine-thirty p.m., on May 10th, it is alleged that you committed the act of second-degree murder. How does the defendant plead?"

"Not guilty," the defense attorney said.

Whitney looked at Shon and back at the defendant, whose name didn't ring a bell with her. When she turned to face Shon again to ask if she knew the person, her face was stone, her eyes spilling a steady stream of tears.

"Your Honor, in light of the severity of the crime, the People are requesting the defendant be remanded without bail," Weiss, the assistant DA, stated.

The defense attorney stood. "Under what grounds? My client is a family man, who owns a business and has a job; with legitimate ties to the community I might add. There is no reason he should be held without the opportunity to post bail."

The judge removed her glasses. "I agree with the defense, Counselor. I see no need to hold him."

"Well, I do, Your Honor," the ADA rebutted. "The defendant's violent past, including several domestic violence reports, weapons possessions, immigration status, and the seriousness of the crime means he is a threat to society, and we cannot risk his return to the community."

"This is nonsense. The prosecution is attempting to punish my client for offenses that occurred more than a decade ago. My client and his wife have attended counseling and mended their relationship. He hasn't had so much as a parking ticket in the past thirty-six months."

"Your client has also only been a legal citizen of the United States for the past five years. That makes him a flight risk, given the brutal nature of the crime, and by the time the trial is over and he's found guilty, there's also a possibility that he will be deported. Shall we keep that on the table?" the prosecution argued.

The defense was pissed but also fully aware of the possibility of deportation. He whispered to his client, whose face showed uncertainty.

The judge denied bail and scheduled the pretrial hearing. Once the assistant DA wrapped up, Whitney called him over. "Hey, what's the deal with that case."

"We found evidence that links him to the murder of Rohan Jackson Garland a few months back."

Whitney's brows furrowed, her eyes widened. She grasped her neck and rubbed her chest. She turned and took Shon's hand and led her to the nearest bathroom. She hadn't known they had arrested someone for Jackson's murder. She could only imagine the turmoil her friend was going through after having just come face to face with the man accused of killing her twin brother.

"Shon, I am so sorry! I never would have brought you into this had I known he was going to be here," Whitney said.

Shon wiped her nose with the tissues she'd found in Whitney's belongings. "It's not your fault. I guess I could have been more persistent in keeping you updated."

"Wait, you knew about this?" Whitney's sympathy waned and she was now offended.

"Only since late last week, when the detectives called my parents to tell them they had come across some evidence, and they were bringing a suspect in for questioning. They asked us to come to the station and look at pictures to see if we knew him or if he looked familiar."

"And you didn't think that was something you should've shared with me?" Whitney was upset, but it only served as a bodyguard to the real emotions she was experiencing: hurt and betrayal.

"I planned to. I had so much going on the other day when you called that I never got around to it. Plus, you've had your head so deep in Chench's crotch that I've barely seen you unless it was work related."

"You're kidding, right? I always answer when you call. You could have tried harder to let me know."

"Well, shit, you work here. I thought maybe you knew already."

"Shon, that's bullshit and you know it. If the detectives called you first then it hadn't even made it to my office." Whitney shook her head and turned around. Her heart was bruised and she wiped the evidence from her eyes. "I can't believe you kept something like this from me. I paid for the entire funeral, plot, and gravestone. Worked at a place that I was less than passionate about just to honor my friend, got close to his sister to have a part of him in my life, only to be shut out by the same person I've come to care about just as much as I cared for him."

"So, now you want to throw it in my face, my family's face? Tell me, Whit, did you do all those things for recognition or self-gratitude? I'm thinking you did it to feel better about the fact that it was the first time you did something for someone other than yourself. I can't believe your ass."

"And I can't believe you! How dare you insult me this way? Jackson was a great friend to me, probably one of the most sincere and consistent people I've ever encountered. I did those things because I cared about *him*, and I wanted him to have a nice farewell, without his family having to beg, borrow, and stea—" Whitney stopped herself before saying the final word. She knew she was jabbing below the belt but only because she was hurt. "You know what, forget it. You did what you did because you felt I was hard to get ahold of, whatever. I won't be in need your services anymore."

"Good, because I won't be providing them anymore, either." Shon pushed the accordion file into Whitney's chest and walked out.

Whitney placed the file on top of her rolling file cabinet and exited the courtroom.

What she thought would be just another day in court had turned out to be a work day from hell. Learning that someone had been charged with her best friend's murder was the furthest from her mind when she had shown up for work. There was still a gaping hole in her heart in the spot Jackson once occupied. She hadn't been assigned to the case, and she may have been deemed too inexperienced to try it, but one thing was for sure and two things were for certain—Whitney Bonesteel had what it took to win, and if anyone was going to bring justice to her friend, it was her. There was no way she was going to take no for an answer.

Chapter Twenty-Four

Whitney sat at her workspace, sifting through the details of a new case she was just assigned. She couldn't help but notice that most of the offenders were young men of color. She wondered if they truly were the ones committing the crimes or if they were simply victims of a skewed and unfair justice system. She propped her chin on her hand as she pondered the question she had just asked herself. The voices coming from the hallway caught her attention. She got up when she saw the man she wanted to see.

"Hey, Gary." Whitney flashed her signature smile. "Do you have a moment?"

Gary looked her up and down in delight." For you, I have several. Come on in my office." Gary had been the district attorney since she'd been in law school and his reputation preceded him. He had come to her campus a couple of times to give presentations, and he always managed to have a few straggling senior students at his side.

Whitney walked in behind him and closed the door. "I wanted to talk to you about the Gordon Stellman case. I know Weiss is the assigned prosecutor, but I really would like to be on it, if possible." Whitney watched Gary look into the air as if trying to recall the particulars. "The one where the guy is being charged for the murder of Rohan J. Garland."

"Ah, yeah. Weiss ran that by me. The grand jury thought the evidence was barely strong enough, but Weiss is on the fence."

"I think we can bump it up to a hate crime."

"Did you not just hear me say, we barely have enough evidence now? And you think we can pile on more charges?"

"Yes, I do. And I have an angle. I just need permission to have the case. If not, then maybe I can be co-counsel with Weiss."

Gary looked at Whitney, placing his hands behind his head and leaning back in his seat. He liked the confidence she exhibited, and it made her even more attractive. "Can you show me one good reason why I should let that happen?"

Whitney didn't have a problem using sex to get what she wanted, but she did have a problem with being seen as a sex object by those in power, expecting her to prove she was capable.

"No, but I can *tell* you why. I'm that damn good!" Whitney gave him a brief rundown of her success stories and stood up. She used her hands to wipe away the crinkles in her skirt. "I look forward to your approval on this case, sir." She turned slowly, giving him an extended view of her backside before switching her hips and strutting slowly out of his office.

By the time she made it back to her desk, the secretary had placed three call slips near her phone. She went to pick one up and saw her father's name on her screen. She started to ignore him again, as she had done many times since their last encounter, but she needed him and decided against it.

"This is Whitney. How can I help you?"

"Wow, I'm shocked you answered. I didn't think—"

"This is Whitney. How can I help you?" she repeated.

"Look, Skittles. I know you're still upset with your mother and me, but we were only trying to protect you. Now, I know we haven't been the best parents, but we weren't the worst, either. Your mother and I worked hard to give you a good life. We don't deserve the way you've been treating us."

"Father, what can I do for you?"

"I beg your pardon? Don't start that shit with me, young lady. You've been calling me Daddy, and you better continue. If you want to play that game, I can and will play it better by redacting you right out of my—."

"Whoa, Daddy, chill out! There's no reason to talk like that." Whitney didn't care how much money she made from her sponsorships; there was no way she was going to allow her father to exclude her from something that was rightfully hers, especially now that there was another beneficiary.

Frederick smiled with victory. He knew how to speak her language and he was more fluent than she gave him credit for. "Oh, good. Glad you caught your sense. Now listen, Pa and Ma are moved into their new place. The house finally sold so I just wanted you to know."

"Good, because as you know I wasn't interested," Whitney said curtly. Glad he wasn't calling to ask her to take it instead.

"I figured it would go to a good owner eventually." Frederick admitted.

"Why don't you ask your other daughter?" Whitney poked. "I'm sure she and her child wouldn't mind a permanent roof over their heads!" When Frederick didn't seem surprised by her statement, it pissed her off. "You knew she had a child, didn't you?"

"How's work going?" Frederick asked, changing the subject.

Whitney wasn't bringing it up because she cared; she was trying to gauge how much Frederick knew.

He knew his daughter well, and there wasn't much she didn't pick up on. She had always been that way since he could remember. The slightest change in behavior, communication, or energy spiked her senses. She was almost always on point. The less he talked about the situation with her, the less he would reveal what he knew about his other daughter.

Whitney was fuming inside. Her father had admitted by omission that he was in touch with his other child and it pissed her off that he was being evasive and dismissive. She had half his DNA, and if he wanted to play that game, she would, too! "Work is good. Actually, not so good. I've been trying to get approval to work on a particular case."

"Did you talk to your boss about it?"

"Yes, I did, but I get the feeling he doesn't think I'm ready. Yet, he basically implied that I could convince him otherwise if I agreed to his inappropriate proposition."

"Your boss, *the DA*, Gary Manilow, was inappropriate with you?"

Whitney confirmed.

"I'm sure he'll give you the okay by close of business tomorrow." Frederick fared his daughter well.

Whitney disconnected the call and made a few calls of her own, two for business and one, personal. By the time she left work, she had secured a follow-up visit with her attorney and Chench. She asked her lawyer to draw up a joint business contract that would have them sharing ownership, but not fifty-fifty, she needed an edge. Just in case Chench got wind of what she was doing and tried to sabotage her efforts, she would have the upper hand. She couldn't risk him going soft and catering to the feelings of his ex-lover. Once the lawyer prepared the contract, she printed it from work and headed to meet Chench. It was about time she got what she needed from him so she could proceed with her plans.

Chapter Twenty-Five

The half-consumed scotch on the rocks that sat on the coffee table had morphed into a watered-down mixture. The ice had melted and the line that Whitney had sniffed gave her a euphoric reaction. When Chench had texted her to tell her he was on his way, she cut her soaking time short. She quickly lathered in her favorite body wash and turned on the shower to wash it away. She didn't bother with clothes because what she had planned when he arrived didn't require any. She needed Chench as comfortable as possible when she presented the paperwork and she knew her nudity would help.

Whitney went to her closet and located her silk robe with the high side splits that she had purchased during her senior class trip to Paris. She sprayed her favorite perfume on her pulse points and moisturized her skin. When Chench rang the bell, her sexy appearance and the smirk she wore let him know that she didn't have much talking in mind. Whitney pulled Chench into the house, closed the door, and made sure all the locks were secure. Chench grabbed her around the waist as Whitney removed his clothing. She rubbed his bare chest and admired his physique. She could tell he spent a lot of time working out. His arms, back, and abs were in great shape, and she loved how his beige complexion enhanced every curve in his upper body. The tattoos were a bonus.

"Damn, it's like that?" Chench asked.

Whitney didn't respond. She continued rubbing his upper body and kissing on his neck and even pecked his lips a few times. She walked over to the kitchen counter and got on top. She opened up her robe and exposed her bare skin.

"Damn!" Chench muttered.

Whitney propped her left leg up on the counter and leaned back on her hands. Chench didn't need to be told what she wanted. He squatted in front of her so his mouth met her lady parts.

"Mmm, that's right, baby. Lick kitty!" Whitney moaned.

She enjoyed the masterful skills Chench seemed to naturally possess. His tongue was like a paintbrush, and her fore and nether regions were his canvass. His strokes sent her into a state of pure bliss and, lately, she'd been hoping she'd have access to his expertise for a lifetime.

When she felt her leg shaking, she pulled his face further into the fork in her thighs and gently grinded. "Yes, please, baby." Whitney begged. She needed him to keep going. She didn't have to advise him on speed or technique because his skills were impeccable. She moved her hand from his head and teased both her nipples. When her orgasm was approaching, she tried pushing him away, but his neck muscles were stronger than the ones in her arm and he stayed put. “Stop, please. I’m cumming … a lot … so haaaarrd,” Whitney screamed, arching her back.

Chench didn’t wait for her to stop trembling before he picked her up and carried her to the bedroom. He laid her on the bed and removed his pants. He climbed on top of the bed, prepared to enter her, when she stopped him. She directed him to lie on his back and proceeded to return the oral favor. When Chench was as hard as he could get, she retrieved a condom from her bedside table and used her mouth to put it on. Chench frowned, impressed, and grabbed ahold of Whitney’s hips as she eased on top of him, rocking and grinding, while licking on his nipples and his lips.

She turned her body 180 degrees while keeping him inside. She rode him in her favorite position, simultaneously fondling his balls. She sucked her middle finger and used it to play with the rim of his anus. He squeezed his muscles and jerked backward. “Trust me,” Whitney said. The tone and sexiness of her words and the pleasure of her movements made Chench ease up. Whitney didn’t penetrate him, but she did rub and massage his rim and balls while clenching her Kegels. When she brought Chench to his completion, she stayed on top of him until he tapped her ass.

“Keep fucking me like that, and I ain’t neva leaving.”

“Keep eating me like that, and you ain’t got to worry about ever leaving,” Whitney confessed.

She locked eyes with Chench and could tell she had him right where she needed him. She went and washed off and brought back a wet cloth for him to do the same.

"I got good news. The lawyer drew up our joint business contract for Moneyworx. Sure you're ready for this?" she asked him.

"Hell yeah. I'm always down to earn clean money." He stood up and put on his boxers.

"Good!" Whitney got out of bed and retrieved some papers from her briefcase. These are the documents. Go ahead and look them over and sign everywhere your name is printed."

"Did you read them?"

"Of Course, I did. I never sign anything without looking it over thoroughly. I suggest you do the same."

"If you checked it out then I know we good. I trust you." Chench looked in her eyes, hoping she felt his words. "I *can* trust you, right?"

This is too easy. "Of course, you can. I have a stake in this, too."

He placed a kiss on her cheek. "Then show me where to sign."

Whitney allowed a smirk to spread across her face. Chaianne may have won the battle, but she planned to win the war and Chench had proven to be an amazing general. Getting him to buy into her plan was much easier than she'd thought. Now, she just had to make their investment offer so attractive that Chaianne would agree, too.

Chapter Twenty-Six

As Whitney juggled a cup of tea in one hand and her rolling cart with the other, the ringing cellphone in her handbag was all it took to cause her anxiety to skyrocket. She sucked in a few deep breaths and mentally and emotionally prepared herself. Today was the first day of Jackson's trial, which had slowly garnered lots of media attention. The LGBTQ community had brought all kinds of awareness to the case.

By the time Whitney switched hands and retrieved her phone, it had stopped ringing. She entered her lock code and checked the missed call log. A text message popped up: *Hey, it's Daddy. Make sure you breathe, kiddo. You're going to do great. Sorry I couldn't be there to watch you open. I'm rooting for you, Skittles. Love you, Dad!*

Whitney took a few more deep breaths and entered the courtroom. The first person she locked eyes with was Shon. Since they hadn't spoken since their fight, she nodded and offered a sincere, empathetic smile and Shon did the same.

Whitney had barely set her stuff down, when Weiss spoke. "You think you're ready for the big league? These aren't low-level, blue-collar offenses. This is a 'go hard or go home' kind of pony show."

Whitney gave him a look. “I’m here, aren’t I?”

“All rise!” The bailiff announced to the courtroom. “Court is now in session.”

Three seconds later, Judge Brandon told them, “You may be seated.”

“Good, ’cause you’re on!” Weiss told Whitney right before the judge addressed the court.

“Good morning, ladies and gentlemen. Calling the case of the People of the State of New York versus Gordon Stellman. Are both sides ready?” Judge Brandon asked.

“Ready for the People, Your honor,” Whitney answered.

“Ready for the Defense, Your honor,” stated Stellman’s attorney.

“Please swear in the jury,” Judge Brandon instructed.

When the bailiff was done, Whitney stood to present her opening statement to the court, laying out a simple overview of the case.

“Your Honor, and ladies and gentlemen of the jury, I will prove to the court that the defendant, Gordon Stellman, not only took a life, but he stole a man from his family and friends. Rohan Garland wasn’t bludgeoned to death out of fear or self-defense nor for protection. He was bashed over the head and strangled in cold blood because of shame, guilt, and embarrassment. I will show the court that Mr. Garland was brutally murdered because the defendant wanted to keep his homosexual indiscretions a secret. I will prove, beyond a reasonable doubt that the only reason the beloved Rohan Jackson Garland was a victim of a fatal *hate crime* was because his sexuality caused another man to question his own."

"Objection!" the defense attorney, shouted. "The decision to charge my client with a hate crime should have been discussed at the pretrial."

"Only if the decision had been made at that time," Whitney countered.

"Your Honor," Bueller pleaded.

"Ms. Bonesteel is correct. New discoveries don't have to be proposed at the pretrial if they weren't established by that date. Absentee motions can be submitted within the specified timeframe between the pretrial and trial, and I believe we..." Judge Brandon looked down at the papers in front of him. "Yup, we received the paperwork on the 12th of this month."

Bueller checked his documents. He was visibly upset when his paralegal pointed to the information on one of the pages. "Dammit," he said under his breath.

When Whitney heard his verbal frustrations, she knew she had him just where she wanted him. She went on to finish her opening statement, uninterrupted and patiently waited for the defense to do the same.

When Judge Brandon announced that it was time to call her first witness, she called the first officer on the scene the day of the crime. “Officer Mahoney, can you please tell the court what you saw when you arrived at the scene of the crime?”

“There was a young, African American male lying on the side of the road, with what appeared to be blunt force trauma to his head.”

“Was there anything found that could’ve served as the weapon used to attack Mr. Garland?”

“Yes, about twenty feet from the victim’s body, we found a tire iron. We bagged it and sent it to the lab. The blood on the weapon matched that of the victim.”

“Mm hm, and did any other matches come back?”

“Yes, the defendants DNA was also on the murder weapon.”

Whitney thanked the officer and informed the judge that she had no further questions.

Bueller replaced her in front of the stand to cross examine. The most he was able to gather in his client’s defense was that the defendant’s DNA wasn’t the only DNA found on the tire iron.

Whitney’s next witness was the medical examiner. “Doctor, can you please tell the people of the court the exact cause of death?”

“Certainly. We concluded that the impact from Mr. Garland’s blunt force trauma to the head was equivalent to him falling headfirst from a three-story building. Although the injury itself didn't cause his death, the results of the impact did. There are three layers that compose the brain: the outer table or the hard layer of bone, the inner layer, which is another layer of bone, and the spongy bone layer called diploe. In the victim's case, the top two layers caused the protective bones to break loose from the skull and pierce the cranium, resulting in damage to the nerve cells."

"And besides the injury from being struck by the tire iron, was there anything else you picked up during the exam?"

"Yes, we saw that there was some bruising and inflammation to his esophagus, which is consistent with something being forced down his throat."

"Could, perhaps, an erect penis cause such bruising and inflammation?"

The doctor's face flushed. "Yes, rough oral sex has been known to cause the same symptoms."

"No further questions." Whitney took her seat.

After hours of back and forth with police officers and the medical examiner, Whitney felt she had performed well. Apparently, her co-counsel thought so, too. "Not bad for a rookie's first day on the floor," Weiss said before smirking and walking away.

Whitney smiled back and packed up her files. She turned to leave, and Shon walked toward her.

"Great job, today. I didn't know you had the case."

Whitney nodded. “Yeah, I just got approval to work on it yesterday, well, right before I got off work. Good thing I went ahead and prepared for it anyway.”

“No shit?” Shon was shocked that she had performed so well, given the lack of preparation time. “Look, about that day. I’m really sorry about how everything went down. I should have put forth more effort to tell you.”

“It’s okay, really. I cared about Jackson, but he was your twin brother. I’m sure it wasn’t easy to keep bringing it up or having to talk about it. I should have been more understanding. That comment about the family not having the money was way out of line. I know that now. I found a new therapist and my first appointment is next Thursday. When I said that to you, I knew I was coming from a place of cruelty. Between Mother, Daddy, Jackson, Patrick, and this pop-up sibling of mine, I’ve been feeling myself slip into a dark space. I don’t want to be there again.” Whitney stepped on the other side of the swing door. “Look, Shon, I did everything out of care and concern. Jackson was a dear friend of mine, and I wanted to help any way I could. There was no self-centered intent.”

“I know that, Bones. We’re women, and our emotions were probably just running high. I know mine were. I’m overwhelmed, under stimulated, and completely fuckstrated.”

Whitney released a laugh. “That’s because you choose to be. I know exactly what you need, too!” Whitney smiled and looked at Shon. “Are we good now?”

Shon hugged her. “Never been better.”

“Good, because I was just starting to *really* like you.” Whitney smiled.

She grabbed her friend around the shoulders and walked toward the door with her. Some things either felt good or they felt right. Today, Whitney had experienced both. Making amends with Shon felt good, but something about prosecuting this case just felt too *right*.

Chapter Twenty-Seven

The new young, black female attorney was creating a stir on all the local news channels. Word had gotten out about how Whitney was dominating the courts, and, as if the case itself weren't enough to garner coverage, her courtroom performance had heightened people's interest. When Whitney walked through the doors, even she was taken aback by how full the room was. In addition to Jackson's family, the defendant's supporters, news reporters, public observers, a lot of other extras filled the gallery. When she walked to her side of the room, she heard whispers and hushed chatter. She asked Weiss what was going on.

"Have you had your head in the sand the last few days, or were you that busy preppin' to kick ass on this case?" he poked at her.

She crinkled her face with confusion. "A little of both."

Weiss showed her the daily paper's headline: "New Attorney at DA's Office Dominating the Legal Scene."

"And they ain't talkin' about me," he confirmed. "We're almost at the finish line. Take us home!" He raised his fist and Whitney bumped it with hers.

This was the moment she had been waiting for, the moment to prove her case, beyond reasonable doubt, and lay out everything that pointed to the defendant's guilt. Whitney called Stellman's coworker to the stand and waited for him to be sworn in before she began.

"Joseph Goosey, can you please share with the court what happened on the night of the incident?"

"Stellman and I had just completed our final delivery of the night. We were driving on Broadway, headed back to the garage, when the front passenger tire began to wobble. I got out first to look things over. It appeared that one of the lugs was loose, so I asked Gordon to get the tire iron from the toolbox and bring it to me. When he got out the truck to do so, that's when the victim approached us. He and Gordon walked off, and when Gordon returned, he told me the guy needed to call a cab, but he didn't have his phone on him, so Gordon loaned him his."

Whitney addressed the jury. "Phone records show that no calls were placed to a cab company that night from the defendant's cell phone. Actually, there were no calls placed from the defendant's phone within that timeframe. I would also like to point out that Mr. Stellman's phone records show that he's been in contact with the victim even before the night of his death. " She turned back to the witness. "And then what happened?"

"I tightened the loose lug, and the thing snapped on me, so I threw it behind me in some bushes. We got back into the truck and headed to the garage to clock out for the night."

"So, you are saying the tire iron never made it back into the work truck?"

"Yes, that's correct. It was broken, so I saw no use for it."

Whitney nodded and moved on to her next point. "According to your employer's records, you punched out at 8:27 p.m., with Stellman right behind you at the same time. Do you remember him leaving with you?"

"Yes, I do. We were parked right next to each other that night. I pulled out of the parking lot and made a right. He pulled out and made a left, headed in the direction of his wife's job."

"That was also the direction where you and the defendant encountered the victim; is that correct?"

"Yes, that is correct."

"No further questions." Whitney exchanged places with Weiss so he could question the witness.

Weiss stood. "Mr. Goosey, please confirm where you and the defendant stopped to tighten the tire lug."

"We were right in front of the empty lot across from the Broadway Laundromat."

"Mm hm," Weiss stated. "Are you sure about that?"

"Yes, I am, because I remember looking at the store to see if they were open, so I could grab some smokes and play my numbers before heading home, but they weren't."

"Thank you. Ladies and gentlemen of the jury, I would like to present Exhibit F." He showed the jury a picture of where the witness said they had stopped to address the tire issue and where the victim's body was found. "As we heard from Officer Mahoney's testimony, the victim's body was found on the other side of the road, about ten feet away from the murder weapon, opposite of where they had stopped and the tire iron was found." Weiss held up an evidence bag containing the weapon that was taken from the scene by law enforcement. "Is this the same tire iron you used and tossed in the vacant lot?"

The witness nodded. "Yes, that's it."

Gasps from both sides permeated the court room. The reporters copiously took notes.

"The People have no further questions," Weiss stated.

Bueller stood to perform his cross examination.

"Mr. Goosey, you were present during the entire exchange between the victim and my client. Is that correct?"

"Yes, it is."

"And how would you describe the interaction between my client and the victim?"

"The victim appeared to be a little agitated with Gordon. When he returned to the truck, I asked Gordon what that was about, and he said it was because he couldn't get an answer from the numbers he had dialed."

"Is it possible, based on his agitated demeanor, that the victim was the aggressor, causing my client to defend himself?"

"Yes, that's possible. When Gordon walked away, heading back toward the truck, I heard the victim yell something. I just couldn't make out what it was."

"Thank you. No further questions."

Whitney called the defendant's wife to the stand. "Mrs. Stellman, can you tell us what your work schedule is?"

"I work Monday through Friday, from noon to nine at night, with an hour lunch break."

"Thank you. On the night of May 10th, do you remember what time you clocked out?"

"Not the exact time. I'm usually out by nine, though."

Whitney grabbed some papers from her table. "Ladies and gentleman of the jury, I would like to present work timesheets for the defendant's wife that show her punch-out time on the day of the incident. I would like to show that Stellman did, in fact, have more than enough time to link up with the victim, commit the crime, and still make it to get his wife from work on time." Whitney handed the paperwork to the judge for review. "The defendant clocked out of work at 8:27 p.m. His wife didn't punch out until 9:25 p.m. Google Maps shows that it typically takes approximately twenty-five minutes to get from the defendant's place of employment to his wife's job. So, there was enough time between the defendant's departure from work and his arrival at his wife's job for an encounter with the victim. Now, Mrs. Stellman did supply a statement to authorities that her husband had picked her up 'on time,' as he does every night, and he was outside her job waiting on her until she got off. I would like to point out that confirmation of whether the defendant was waiting outside of his wife's job for twenty-plus minutes is questionable. In this case, the use of the term 'on time' is nothing more than an assumption. Yes, he may have been on time because when Mrs. Stellman walked out, he was there, waiting. But she can't positively attest to the fact that her husband had been waiting outside of her job since nine p.m. In fact, I know she can't, because surveillance cameras from the neighboring building show the defendant pulling up in front of his wife's job exactly 180 seconds before his wife exited the building, and he was wearing something different than the maroon polo-style work shirt that he'd worn when he left his job."

Whitney walked to her table and retrieved the remote. She turned on the monitor and played two videos of the defendant: one of him wearing his employer-issued work shirt as he walked out of his job on the day of the murder and another of him wearing a plain t-shirt when he'd arrived at his wife's job.

She pressed a couple more buttons and a different video emerged on the monitor. It showed Stellman pulling up to his wife's job, exiting his car, and placing a bag into the trash bin on the corner. "We were unable to track down the garbage collected from that container, but we believe the work shirt, stained with the victim's blood, was in that bag, which explains why the defendant didn't have it on when he arrived to pick up his wife."

"Objection, hearsay." Bueller said.

"Sustained," Judge Brandon announced. "The jury will disregard the prosecutor's last statement."

Whitney looked over at the defendant and then his wife. There was something about the pendant around his wife's neck that caught her attention. As much as she wanted to ignore it, it kept flashing in her mind. She had seen it before and was hell bent on finding out where.

"Mrs. Stellman, have you ever known your husband to watch pornography?"

"Well, um ..."

"The court would like to remind the witness that she is under oath," Whitney warned.

"Yes, he has in the past, but he doesn't any longer," she stated confidently.

"Have you known your husband to watch homosexual pornography?"

Mrs. Stellman frowned in disapproval. “Of course not. Gordon isn’t attracted to men!”

“People of the jury, I would like to present Exhibit G.” Whitney turned over the evidence. “This document shows the various websites visited by the defendant six months prior to May 10th, right up until his arrest.” Whitney retrieved another piece of paper. “Exhibit H also shows a list of pay-per-view porn videos, such as *Big Black Cocks*, *He Bangs*, and *Meaty Mayhem,* to name a few, obtained from his cable bill. All of these titles indicate Mr. Stellman’s homosexual interests.”

Mrs. Stellman’s face turned ashen and her lips quivered. She never even looked in her husband’s direction.

“No further questions.” Whitney walked away with a delicate smirk.

~~~

Monday was closing statements, and Whitney couldn’t let go of the image of the pendant Mrs. Stellman wore around her neck. It was subtle, but the shape, size, and color were unmistakable. As she sat, wondering why she was so fixated, a tap at the door broke her concentration.

“Guess you were right all long.” Gary stood in front of the conference room door. He walked in and sat down next to her. “Late nights make productive days in the courtroom, I see.”
~~~

"Yes, seems that way. Had some other stuff to go over before tomorrow."

"You're brighter than I gave you credit for. I didn't think you were ready to take on a case of this magnitude but, apparently, someone thought you were." He leaned in closer to Whitney and touched the tips of her hair. "I wonder what you can show me that will give me that much confidence in you as well." He touched her behind the neck.

Whitney maneuvered her body out of his grasp. "How can I help you?"

"I've seen you firsthand, and I want to acknowledge your success. How about we stop at the pub and have a celebratory drink?"

"How about we not and you just state your compliments right here." Whitney stared him in the eye.

Gary stood over Whitney. "So, you're one of those feisty black women, right? The kind whose momma headed the feminist movement?"

Whitney stood, too. She was just about to address her boss in the most insubordinate way, when Weiss showed up. "Oh, there you are! I went to your desk, but you weren't there. A few of us are heading to the pub for a drink. Care to join us?" He saw Whitney was about to decline and spoke again. "Come on! You've been kicking ass in the courtroom all week. You have the whole weekend to rest. Plus, you know you got this, and you can do Monday's closing argument in your sleep."

Whitney looked at her dickhead boss and her very attractive co-counsel and reasoned that if she was going to spend her time with someone, it wasn't going to be Gary.

Whitney looked at her watch and figured she had a little time to spare before her appointment with Chaianne. "Okay, an hour tops!" She gathered her items and walked out of the office, leaving her boss standing there, fuming from the ears.

Chapter Twenty-Eight

Whitney had rushed home to shower and change before her meeting with the owner of Private EyE. The wig she'd purchased would help hide her identity in addition to the oversized shades she planned to wear. She had to be careful to use a different voice to further maintain her disguise. If Chaianne was half as keen as Whitney and their father, there was a chance she would easily see past the facade, especially since she and Whitney had more than enough run-ins. Whitney's sole purpose for using Chaianne's company was so she could see firsthand if her business was worth the time and energy she was putting into forming MoneyWorx. Whitney wanted to take something Chaianne had worked hard to build and destroy it from the inside, the same as Chaianne's presence had done to her relationship with her father. If she could gain access to Chai's company, Whitney's plan was to bankrupt it or have Chaianne eternally indebted to her.

Finding a parking spot close to the coffee shop was proving to be a difficult challenge. It had practically rained all day, and the moisture in the air had Whitney almost ready to throw in the towel, until she saw a car pulling out. She quickly reversed into the space and hurried toward their meeting spot.

She was almost fifteen minutes late and, after going through all the trouble, she hoped Chaianne was still there. When she walked through the doors, she noticed how Chaianne was looking at her, probably questioning her choice in style, and she immediately felt uncomfortable.

"Hi. Are you Annette?" Whitney asked. That was the name Chaianne had on her business card so that's the name Whitney used.

"Yes, and I take it you're Mrs. ..."

"Oh yes, Mrs. Robinson."

"Please, have a seat," Chaianne offered.

She was much more pleasant than what Whitney was used to, which almost made her question her decision.

Once Whitney was seated and comfortable, Chaianne spoke again. "So, please tell me the reason for your inquiry."

Wow! She's so professional. I like that! "My husband and I have been married for fifteen years," she started, but then paused when Chaianne glanced at her ring finger, which was sans a ring. "Oh, I'm not wearing it and after I'm done talking, you will know why."

Whitney had already rehearsed the Grammy worthy storyline and performance she hoped would convince Chaianne that she was who she claimed to be. Now was her time to perform. She continued. "For the first ten years, we were in pure bliss. My husband spoiled me to no fault. He told me that I never had to work, and he treated me like a queen.

Five years ago, my doctor told me I may never get pregnant, and that was when things turned sour. He started ‘working late,’ lying about his whereabouts, taking ‘business trips’ all the time, and turning his phone off whenever he was in the house with me. For a while, I assumed he was just not happy about me being infertile. But eventually, his behavior seemed more like that of a cheating spouse than a disgruntled husband. It got really bad when this woman began calling the house and asking for him by name.” Whitney dabbed her eyes for emotional effect.

Chaianne reached into her bag and handed Whitney a tissue.

“I’m sorry to be crying like this. I-I just don’t know what to do anymore. I love him so much, and it will kill me if we break up. I just need proof that he’s cheating: videos, pictures, recordings, anything you can get.” Whitney slid a card across the table. “Here is my contact information. Please mail your findings as soon as you can.”

Chaianne asked a few more questions and as soon as she was done, Whitney got up and walked out. Getting back at Mitch and using Chaianne’s business to do it didn’t give her a good feeling. She had witnessed firsthand just how crazy Mitch was, and her gut told her that things may not go so smoothly. Mitch was known to be jealous and possessive and willing to annihilate anything or anyone who got in his way. Therefore, Whitney hoped her plan would allow her to gain financial access to Chaianne's company and punish her for the physical assaults. That's why she decided to have the findings sent to Mitch's home. Once he found out who was behind his wife wanting to leave him, she knew he'd act. A small part of her felt bad for having done it, but she rationalized it by reminding herself of the times Chaianne had beat her up. *Let's see how tough she is when she has to defend herself*, Whitney mused.

Even though Chaianne seemed like a nice person, sincerely interested in helping "Mrs. Robinson" get the truth, it wasn't enough to make Whitney change her mind. Chaianne was unwanted, unwelcomed, and at this point, her actions were unforgivable. She had violated and disrespected Whitney one too many times; as far as Whitney was concerned, she deserved what lay ahead.

~~~

Whitney awoke to Chench standing on her side of the bed, looking down at her. She must have been in a deep sleep because she hadn't even heard him enter the house, let alone her bedroom. After meeting with Chaianne, Whitney tried contacting Chench to come keep her company, but he didn't answer her calls or texts, so she ended up going to bed alone. Since meeting him, her desire to be with sponsors had waned and although she missed out on a lot of money, she felt like Chench's presence made her richer. She quietly craved his
~~~

company, secretly desired his touch, and candidly requested his sex. She was surprised that she had allowed herself to open up to someone like him. She had come across plenty of doctors, lawyers, CEOs, Wall Street Execs and, of course, her fair share of law enforcement officers, but none had captured her attention the way a street hustler named Chench had. She was so into him that after he signed the paperwork that night, she offered him a spare key and he gladly accepted it. Until now, she didn't have a reason to second guess her decision.

"It's ten o'clock. How long you gonna sleep?" He glared at the small mound of white powder next to her side of the bed. "I think it's time you give that shit a rest."

She looked too and rolled her eyes. "Did you come here to argue? If so, I have better things you can do with your tongue and my time."

She had quickly learned that Chench was controlling and most times it turned her on, but now wasn't one of them. Whitney was used to having the power in her relations and she was rarely controlled by others. Her personality was so dominant that she secretly desired to be submissive. And although she didn't mind Chench's domineering demeanor, what she couldn't take was his argumentative side. That was something she just didn't care to do.

"Yeah, whatever. I know you betta not been giving my pussy away. I drove by and your car wasn't here." He reached under the covers and felt between her legs. The moistness down there caused an instant erection. He began to undress so he could take a shower. “Why you gotta go out of town again?”

“I told you this was a vacation I had planned since last year. Jackson and I were supposed to go, and now I’m taking Shon.”

Chench looked at her with the lust of a hundred men. “Yeah, aiight. If you say so. You better not be doing no shit you ain’t got no business.”

“Oh, you mean the shit that you do?”

“Whatever. You be acting like you don’t want me but talking like you do. You stay sending mixed messages, and that ain’t cool.”

“I gave you a key to my place. If that isn’t a clear message that you’re welcome here, then I don’t know what is.”

“Yeah, but I want to be welcomed here too,” Chench touched her chest above her heart.

Whitney wasn’t a jealous woman and understood that attraction to other people was a normal occurrence amongst the human species. Based on how she’d met Chench, she all but knew he had other women in his life; but refused to stress him about it seeing as how she’d been living her life. On the other hand, Chench was as jealous as they came and would never agree to let her go on this trip if he knew what she had planned. It was the bachelor party for one of her sponsors, and there was a lot of money to be made that night.

Whitney joined Chench in the shower, where she proceeded to give him the longest and wettest blowjob to date. It was also the second or third time she allowed him to penetrate her with no protection, and she hoped she wouldn't regret it.

"You know I love you, right?" he asked her.

Whitney continued to rotate her hips while bending at the waist. "Mm hm. But don't talk, just stroke." Whitney loved the way Chench felt inside of her. Every part of her body had met every part of his and she was starting to realize just how much she wanted him around. But she still couldn't bring herself to tell him she loved him and, usually, he was fine with that.

He knew she had love issues, but as long as she made it known that she was going to be a permanent fixture in his life, he would be okay. Unlike his ex-girlfriend, who constantly reminded him of just how disposable he was, he felt secure in his relationship with Whitney, and there wasn't anything he wouldn't do to make her happy. Today must have been different.

"What, am I just a fuck to you?" Chench slid himself out of her.

She stood upright. "No, of course not, Chench. I like you, too."

He turned off the water and stepped out of the shower. "We been fucking around for months now, and I have yet to hear you say you love me back. All the shit I do for you to show how much I care, and all you can say is 'shut up and stroke'?"

"I didn't mean it like that." Whitney grabbed her towel and stepped out, too. "I was just in the moment and …"

"Yeah, I was too and you ruined it."

His facial expressions told Whitney everything she needed to know about how he was feeling. He kept his eyebrows crinkled and his mouth tight. Once he dried off and put back on the same clothes he had just removed, he fared her well.

"I'll talk to you later. I'm out."

"But you just got here. Please don't leave."

He didn't as much look at her as he walked out and left her standing there, wrapped in a towel.

Chapter Twenty-Nine

Feeling lonely and lost, Whitney turned to the only man who had never walked out on her or steered her wrong. Despite how she had been treating him lately, the one person she could always count on was Frederick Bonesteel. He was always there when she needed him and right now, she needed her Daddy. Whitney almost never involved him in her personal life, but after the blowup with Chench, she was desperate for some genuine male guidance. She placed the call and was glad when he answered on the first ring.

"Daddy?" Whitney's voice was shaky.

"Be sure to send them as soon as you can," he said, addressing someone in the background before turning his attention to Whitney. "Skittles, what's wrong? Is everything okay?"

"Yes, I'm fine. I just needed to talk. Listen, I'm sorry for the way I've been acting. It's just that I'm really troubled inside and sometimes I don't know how to process ..."

"Hold on, baby. I just sent the forms via interoffice mail. It should be there any minute," he said to someone else. He refocused on Whitney. "Sorry, it's crazy here today. What were you saying?"

Whitney sighed and rolled her eyes. Work was always top priority for her father and right now, she wished he could make her number one. “Look, if now is not a good time, I can call you back later.”

“You sure? That would be better. Let me get you over to my secretary, and she can put some time on my schedule. Daddy loves you. Talk soon.”

Although she wasn’t happy about having to be placed on her father’s schedule, Whitney realized that was his reality. She waited a few seconds for his secretary to pick up.

“Hi, Whitney. It looks like your dad has some free time tomorrow morning before his nine o’clock briefing. How’s that?”

“Um, yeah, sure. That’s fine.” She was willing to take what she could get.

“Did he tell you the good news?”

“No. What good news?” Whitney asked.

“He was able to get your sister the house his parents used to live in. He dropped the price to make it affordable for her. He is so glad to have family living there,” the babbling secretary revealed.

“Oh, yeah. Wow, that’s great!” Whitney replied, before abruptly hanging up.

She wasn’t sure if she should call her dad back and interrogate him or just leave well enough alone. Clearly, Frederick had a desire to help the child he never had a relationship with, and that was his right, but Whitney also felt like he had an obligation to her to be transparent and he was being everything but. Granted, she hadn't made it easy for him to talk to her about Chaianne, she still felt like he was going about it the wrong way.

She wasn't sure why she'd called him to discuss her man problems anyway. Her father would never approve of her dating someone like Chench. Frederick would have asked about the work history Chench didn't possess and want to know about the criminal history he had. Plus, he had always been vocal about her dating someone from a background like theirs.

Frederick didn't mind interracial dating; he just preferred that his daughter gave men of color a fair shake. She recalled how he had broached the topic not too long ago. "My firm just hired this new employee. Malik is young, handsome, and single. I can introduce you two," he'd said suggestively. When he noticed how bothered Whitney seemed to be, he left it alone.

A part of her wished he'd been that vocal and persistent when sharing information about his other daughter. If Whitney had to guess, she'd say her father was ashamed of his absence in Chaianne's life, which was how she came to live in his parents' old home. Now she wished she had taken the house just so Chaianne couldn't get it.

~~~
~~~

Exasperated and overwhelmed, Whitney entered the office of her new therapist. Grateful that court had been adjourned for the rest of the week, she was glad she could use Friday to tend to her affairs. It had been almost a year since she'd last seen a therapist and the recent myriad of emotions she had been experiencing only confirmed that she had taken the right step in pursuing one. Until that day, things had been going well with Chench, a little too well in her mind. He was merely supposed to serve a purpose but ended up having a presence. Things were changing for Whitney and the internal transformations were still uncomfortable for her.

Shon was proving to be the friend she never realized she wanted, let alone needed. And even though her immediate reaction to Chaianne wasn't the best, Shon was able to shift how she viewed her. However, that was short lived after their violent encounters. Shon and Chench were two people she was embracing more openly than she'd expected, yet she still had cold spots in her heart for people she should've been willing to protect. So here she was, in yet another therapist's office, with suppressed hopes of being made whole. The only difference with this therapist was that she looked more like Whitney—a black woman, who appeared not to take any shorts when it came to delivering the treatment needed to help a black girl lost.

"So," the therapist started, making direct eye contact with little emotion. "Before we start, how do you prefer I address you?"

Taken aback by her direct and proficient approach, Whitney replied, "Whitney is fine."

"I understand I'm your third therapist in eight years and although I don't care to know the details of why your other therapists didn't work, I am interested in finding out what you are hoping to get from these sessions."

Geesh. No smiles, soft introductions, or wall art to offer me a focus point, Whitney thought. She only had the unreadable face of a woman who was clearly qualified to carry out the task at hand based on all the letters after her name. "Well, Dr. Keptin, to be honest, I have issues that I would like to work on. I have this guy in my life that I'm really starting to like ... a lot. Lately, he's been expressing his love for me and I haven't done the same in return. I've never really been in love or knew what it felt like to want to be with someone all the time until I met him. Except, he thinks we met by chance." Whitney looked down to avoid having to look into her eyes. *Damn, where's the wall porn when I need it!*

"How did you meet him? Tell me more about that," Dr. Keptin probed.

"He's the boyfriend of my father's daughter."

"Your sister?"

"My father's daughter," Whitney repeated, trying to make it clear to her new therapist that, by no means, did she plan to recognize that woman as her sibling. "When I found out I had an Irish twin, to say I was pissed is an understatement. I had spent twenty-four years of my life believing I was my parents' only child, only to learn that wasn't the case. Maybe if she was a he, I would have accepted it, but she isn't."

"Why does her gender bother you?"

"I think I see her as competition as opposed to an addition. My relationship with my mother is strained and it's been that way for as long as I can remember. Daddy has always been my happy place. I never cared where he was or who he was with. I felt most loved, accepted, and adored when I was with him. I knew no matter what, no woman could take my place. It was like I was his queen, his princess, and everything in between."

Dr. Keptin said nothing but maintained eye contact. She was waiting on Whitney to admit what she may not have wanted to, which was keeping her from accepting her sister in her life. "Please continue."

Whitney rubbed her neck and patted her chest. "When it came to women, if I wasn't feeling them or if they weren't treating me right, Daddy would stop seeing them. He had even called off an engagement one time because his potential wife and I couldn't seem to make amends and just like that, he ended it."

"What does his relationship with his other daughter have to do with your bond with your father?" Clearly, Whitney needed help getting to her point, so Dr. Keptin continued to dig.

Whitney looked around and then at her therapist. She hadn't said it, nor did she want to admit it. She prided herself on being unbothered by others, especially other women, because her father had made her feel that secure in herself, but this was different. "I just don't like her." Whitney couldn't bring herself to admit the truth.

"Don't like her? Have you met her?"

"No." *At least not officially*.

"So, how can you say you don't like someone you've never met?" Dr. Keptin sat up straighter.

Even though her tone hadn't changed and her expression remained the same, it was something about her disposition that made it clear to Whitney that she was about to hear something she didn't want to.

"Can I be honest here?" It was a rhetorical question. She didn't even wait for Whitney to answer before she started talking again. "I think you see your sister—and I'm going to refer to her as that because that's exactly who she is, whether you choose to admit it or not—as a threat. Her presence intimidates you because you know she isn't like those other women your father would just dismiss and dispose of because you didn't like them. With her, it's different. You're regarded as his baby girl, and the reality of there being two of you bothers you more than her existence. Your father kept her a secret from you for a reason, and I think it's because he knew it would hurt you and he was trying to protect your heart. When we love, we tend to put the feelings of others above our own and we love them when they least deserve it because that's when they need it the most. It's known as unconditional love. Your father has that for you, despite you having interfered with his personal affairs. I believe you are now old enough to provide the same to him. I challenge you to meet her. Introduce yourself and welcome her to the family. Even if you don't become close or buddies, at least you are showing your father that you're finally willing to accept someone in his life other than yourself."

Whitney left Dr. Keptin's office torn between never going back and secretly looking forward to seeing her again. Although she didn't appreciate her assessment, she had to respect her frankness. It was a level of honesty she wasn't ready to face, but something she genuinely needed.

Chapter Thirty

After the entire weekend went by, it became painfully obvious to Whitney that she had hurt Chench in a way she hadn't intended. He hadn't reached out to her, nor had he accepted contact from her. When she left her therapist's office, she had driven by every bar she'd known him to frequent and every home she'd known him to visit but there were no signs of him. Now, as she found herself sitting down the road from the house she once considered her home, she could no longer admit that she didn't have deeper feelings for him than what she led on. Whitney had sat looking at her grandparents' old home for almost an hour and contemplated pulling off, when she saw a man wearing a military uniform walking up the stairs, carrying a child.

Whitney sat up in her seat and started her car. She drove slowly past the house just in time to see Chaianne open the door and let them both in. *At least I know Chench isn't here with her. But where the hell could he be?* Whitney now realized that Chaianne was just as much her competition as she was her enemy. Although her initial disdain for her was due to the multiple attacks, she now also disliked her because both the men she cared about also cared about Chaianne.

That reality was a hard pill for her to swallow, and that was why she didn't feel as bad about the work she was putting in to try and have some sort of hold over Chaianne. Her lawyer told her that the offer was presented to Chaianne and her attorney, the previous week, and that Chaianne was excited about MoneyWorx's interest in her company and the possibility of expanding her business. It was just the confirmation Whitney needed.

Whitney was sitting on the commode, enjoying a magazine, when her cellphone rang, stopped, and then rang again, taking her out of her zone. She stood and waddled to her dresser to get it before heading back into the bathroom to finish her business.

"Hello?" Whitney answered, wondering who could possibly be calling her that late.

There was noise in the background but she did her best to listen to the voice on the other end. "Yo, it's me. They just picked me up on some bullshit. I can't get ahold of my man. Can you come bail me out?"

"Chench?"

"Yeah, who else it's gonna be?"

Well this explains why I haven't heard from him. Whitney rolled her eyes and asked for his location. "I'll be right there."

She cleaned herself up and washed her hands before getting dressed to go see about Chench. Although it took way longer than she'd liked for them to release him, she was glad to see his face once they did. She walked up to him and wrapped him in her arms.

"Are you okay?" she asked as she looked him over.

"Yeah, I'm good. We can talk later. Let's get up outta here."

Once they made it to the car, Chench waited until Whitney drove off to talk. "Yo, I told Dollar and them niggas about fuckin' around with new mufuckas. They little asses always into some shit."

Whitney didn't ask because she didn't want to know specifics. She just let him vent.

"They been hanging around this new dude who ain't street at all and now all of a sudden, they havin' random, unwarranted run-ins with dem boys. Them muhfuckas know I don't do five-o at all."

"What does that have to do with you? How did you end up arrested? Whitney asked.

"We was coming from the bar downtown and got blooped. They must have smelled the couple of beers I had and asked me step out the car."

"Well, were you drunk?"

"Hell no. Well, I didn't feel drunk, but them fucking pigs breathalyzed me anyway and of course, they found a reason to cuff me."

"Did they give you a court date?"

"Yeah, man, in two weeks. I hope I ain't gotta do no time. This like my third DUI in two years. Fuck!"

"Babe, relax. Who was the arresting officer? Do you remember?"

"Some asshole named Yiellow."

Whitney smiled inwardly. She'd had him before and knew just what to do to ensure Chench got off. "I know exactly who you're talking about. Make sure you make it to court. I'll do the rest."

He looked at her with grateful and pleading eyes. "I'ma need you to do one more thing for me. Think you can handle it?"

Whitney thought of all the ways Chench had shown his love for her and now she wanted to return the favor, especially since he had never asked her for anything.

"I guess it depends on what it is." She was still an officer of the law and she wasn't about to risk her livelihood by doing anything too crazy. Her father had always told her, "Pigs get fat and hogs get slaughtered," so she made sure that whatever barely legal things she engaged in were enough to eat without being greedy.

Her reply made Chench proud. "Nothing crazy at all. I just need you to be you."

If that was all he needed, then that she could provide. She needed her energy and nerves to win the case in honor of her best friend and before she knew it, Monday would be arriving sooner than her anxiety could bare.

Chapter Thirty-One

Today was the moment she had to prove her case beyond a reasonable doubt. It was her final opportunity to bring Jackson's killer to justice. Even though she knew a conviction wouldn't bring his family any more closure than a funeral service, she felt she was doing her part to give them the opportunity to move on from this ordeal.

As she waited for court to proceed, Whitney pulled out her cell phone and went through some images of Jackson. She heard people entering the courtroom and looked up and over in enough time to see Mrs. Stellman taking her seat directly behind her husband. When she looked back down at her phone, the photo Jackson had sent her the night of his death was looking back at her. *My God. Shit! I can't believe this was under my nose all this time*.

In the photo Jackson had sent, she could see an image of another person from the neck down in the background. Around the unidentified person's neck was the same pendant the defendant's wife had worn. Upset that there was nothing else she could do, Whitney stood when she felt Weiss nudge her and Judge Brandon call her name. It was time for closing arguments.

"Good morning, ladies and gentlemen of the jury. On the fateful day of May 10, 2005, a crime of ghastly proportions was committed. The defendant, Gordon Stellman, used his size, strength, and a discarded work tool to end Rohan Garland's life. Rohan was a loving son, brother, uncle, and friend. He was an openly proud member of the LGBTQ community, who had relations with someone who closeted his homosexual preference, ultimately leading to Mr. Garland's death. As we've seen from witness testimony and demonstrative evidence, we have proven, beyond a reasonable doubt, that the defendant murdered Mr. Garland in cold blood. His coworker placed the defendant and the murder weapon at the scene of the crime. The defendant's phone records prove that he had contact with the victim prior to the night of his death and moments before his untimely demise. We have proof of Mr. Stellman's secret fetish for homosexual pornography from his cable bill and internet browser history. Time sheets from both the defendant and his wife's places of employment indicate there was more than enough time between his dismissal from work and picking up his wife for him to commit the crime. Surveillance videos show him changing clothes after he'd murdered the victim. Finally, the medical examiner has testified that the victim suffered injuries consistent with invasive oral sex. It is your job, your duty, as members of the jury to deliver justice. On behalf of the State of New York and the brutally slain victim, who no longer has a voice, I ask that you find Gordon Stellman guilty of second degree murder and committing a hate crime against Rohan Jackson Garland. Thank you."

~~~

Praying wasn't usually Whitney's thing, but when she watched the jury walk back into the courtroom, she bowed her head and sent one up on behalf of her deceased friend and his family. She turned and glanced at Shon, hoping her eyes conveyed everything she was unable to say: "I did my best. I gave it my all. I hope I made you all proud."

"All rise," the bailiff announced as the judge reentered the courtroom.

Whitney grabbed her chest. Patted.

"Has the jury reached a verdict?" the judge asked.

Her palms were sweaty. She had won in the courtroom before, but none were as important as this.

The foreman stood. "Yes, Your Honor."

Please, please, say guilty.

"What have you?"

Whitney swallowed hard. She looked back at the faces in the courtroom. Shon and her family looked uneasy. Mrs. Stellman looked frightened. Her daddy was stoic yet proud.

"On count one, the charge of murder in the second degree, we the jury find the defendant, Gordon Stellman,
~~~

guilty. As to count two, the charge of committing a hate crime, we find the defendant not guilty."

Time stopped. The room grew smaller, and although Whitney could see the tears of Jackson's family and feel the shoulder grab from her colleague, she still couldn't believe what she was witnessing was real. She had asked for the case, gotten it, and won on behalf on her friend. Despite the doubt, the long hours, and the sleepless nights, she'd always kept the end goal in mind and gave it everything she had.

"Congratulations, Bonesteel. You did it!" Weiss hugged her even tighter. The sexual energy they'd shared after leaving the bar was still present in her body. Even though she felt bad about stepping out on Chench, knowing how much he was into her, Weiss was the distraction and release she needed to ease the anxiety she'd felt leading up to this moment.

Whitney walked through the sea of supporters, and once outside the courtroom, she stopped to give a brief statement. She thanked the jury for doing their part in bringing the defendant to justice and offered her sympathy to Jackson's family. During the brief interview, she locked eyes with Shon, and as soon as she finished, she walked over to her friend and gave her the biggest hug.

Whitney's dad respectfully interrupted their embrace. "I just want you to know you did one helluva job today. I am so proud of you, and there was never a doubt in my mind that you could win this. Now, it's my turn to step up to the plate and we should talk. I'll be in touch soon." Mr. Bonesteel placed a kiss on his daughter's forehead, shook her friend's hand as well as the rest of the family and stepped away.

Through tears, Shon congratulated her on a job well done. "You did it, bitch! I can't believe you did it!"

Whitney swiped a few tears from her eyes. As much as she thought she was giving up on Jackson by leaving the LGBTQ agency to work for the DA's office, she realized that everything happened for a reason, and she was exactly where she needed to be.

"Thank you so much for believing in me and supporting me throughout this whole ordeal. There were so many times I quietly doubted my ability, and you were right there to reassure me. I appreciate you, Shon."

"Nah, we appreciate you, B to the FF." Shon opened her arms and signaled for her family to come over to greet Whitney. They all stood in a small circle, hugging.

Although prosecution had proven to be a successful move, it had given Whitney a firsthand glimpse into just how fragmented the justice system was. People who couldn't afford private counsel were provided subpar representation by the same attorneys who ate lunch with the people who were trying to put them away. That seemed to be the case for a lot of the inner city, low-income defendants she had to prosecute, simply because their resources were limited, and no one cared. Just because black men didn't meet her requirements for dating didn't mean they didn't deserve proper legal representation from competent and empathetic attorneys. The people of color who were convicted because of her work were no different than Jackson. She couldn't continue to sit idly by as people who looked like her suffered at the hands of a justice system that didn't. At that moment, she realized she couldn't continue to work for the DA too much longer. She wanted to become a public defender.

Chapter Thirty-Two

When Chench had asked Whitney for help, she didn't know it would entail moonlighting as a bartender during her precious weekends off. He said he needed her assistance to find out some things because she was good when it came to reading people and extracting information. She hated that she had to spend time in a place she didn't enjoy to prove her commitment to him.

"Yo, I got the green light from the owner, and you can start next weekend. I told him you were interested in bartending, and he's gonna let you try it out," Chench stated. "All I need you to do is get close with this dude. Gain his trust and ask him about what we talked about." Now it was her time to show and prove.

It was her second day bartending at one of the places she had frequented with Chench, but it was the one she didn't like. He'd told her he would send a picture of the person he needed her to befriend, but she hadn't gotten it yet.

Now, she wondered if every black man who entered the bar was the person she was supposed to be pursuing. Being anonymous wasn't all bad. She enjoyed the visual assessment of the people she normally wouldn't even make eye contact with.

Being around Shon and based on their talks, she was starting to become less rigid in her decision to exclusively date white men. Shon's outlook on the black culture was more positive than Whitney's, and their many talks were starting to open her eyes. So when one black guy walked up, she took notice of just how attractive the "brothas" really were. As soon as he approached the bar, Whitney walked over to him.

"Hey, handsome. Interested in anything in particular?" Whitney said, flirting.

She watched his eyebrow go up as he pondered the weight of her question. "Um, I think so. Give me a second, though."

Whitney took note of his dark skin, long, freshly twisted locs, cut arms, and dreamy eyes, and instantly imagined what he would be like in the bedroom. "I can get you anything you'd like, and I do mean *anything*." She licked her lips for effect. When he didn't respond, she continued. "You here alone?"

"Nah, I'm with my girl."

Whitney scrunched her face in disapproval. "Well, when you're ready to upgrade from shrimp to caviar, come find me." Just as the words left her mouth, a person she didn't expect to see emerged.

"Still interested in other people's men, huh Jasmine?"

Whitney rolled her eyes. *I can't seem to escape this bitch.* "Nope, just yours," she replied to Chaianne. "If the last man was yours, then he wouldn't have been between my legs on the regular, now would he?" She was a safe distance away and had access to bottles for protection, which made her feel comfortable being lippy.

"Bitch, please! You and I both know you couldn't hold an open flame to me. The only reason you got him was because he's always been a sucka for easy pussy. But that's neither here nor there. I don't fuck him or fuck *with* him anymore. Any dick you done had, I don't want. Matter of fact, get me another bartender, bitch, and go shovel shit or something," Chaianne spat.

The other bartender must have heard the exchange and quickly went over to Chaianne to take her order. "I got it," she told Whitney. "Can you please get the guy at the end another Budweiser?"

The two of them made eye contact once more, throwing glares are one another. But Whitney wasn't stupid. She knew that Chaianne's disdain for her was just as strong. Her intuition told her that Chaianne, too, had a breaking point and if Whitney hadn't reached it yet, she was close. There was no telling how far her wrath could reach.

Whitney stayed at the bar for another hour and then texted Chench to let him know she was leaving. She told him she saw no purpose for being there unless she knew who to look out for. He texted her right back and said he was working on getting her a picture and she would have it by the following day. She was beyond pissed and felt like he had wasted an evening on foolishness. On her way home, she placed a call to Shon.

"Girl, you are never going to believe this!" Whitney started.

"Ah shit! What happened now?" Shon replied.

"So, you know Chench got me spying and shit. Well tonight, I was at the bar and in walks this fine-ass black dude."

"Wait, what? Since when are you scoping out the brothas?"

"Since you started bragging about all the men you've encountered and how no one could ever take the place or your "peoples," and the only thing you like dark is your men, and blah blah, blah."

Shon laughed. "Well, it's true! Shit, my daddy is a strong black man, just like my brothers, uncles, and cousins. There's just something dope about our men, and I don't think I could ever commit to anyone of another race."

"See, and it was those conversations that got me thinking and seeing the light. Well ... the night," Whitney joked.

They both laughed.

"So, like I was saying, I was bartending tonight and in walks this fine, dark-skinned man. I mean, Shon, he was so attractive that I would have left with him if he'd let me."

"So, why didn't you push up?" Shon asked.

"I did, and he shut me down. Told me he had a girl, and guess who he was with." Whitney shrieked.

"Who?"

"Chaianne! It's like I can't escape her. She's fucking everywhere. In Daddy's life, Chench's life, the bar, my damn head."

"Damn, how did that encounter go?"

"She didn't attack me, thank God. But, of course, she belittled me and said a few choice words." Whitney replayed the exchange.

"Damn, I don't think y'all will ever get along," Shon admitted. "You know I went on that social site and looked her up. I don't know her personally, but I was pretty cool with her two friends, Chanel and Shakyra in school. She had a fight with my homegirl Vera one time, so I don't think she ever really cared for me too much since then."

"Join the club. She's probably one of those miserable hood rats, who will always hate and be jealous of the next person. Chench told me her mother did some prison time and, of course, we know Daddy never had a relationship with her. She and Chench have broken up, she's not with her daughter's father and now she has a new beau. Who knows how long this will last. Maybe she's bitter."

"Yeah, maybe. But I'll tell you one thing, you better watch your back when you're down there. She don't take too kindly to disrespect and based on what I know, she will go hard for hers. She fucked Vera's ass up for messing with her old dude, Vaughn. And Shakyra and Chanel ride hard for her."

"Damn, now you make me not want to go there anymore. You know I don't do that fighting shit," Whitney said.

"I know, and she does, which is why I'm telling you to be easy with her. Ignore her if you can. Of course if I'm around, I won't let anybody fuck with you, but I'm just saying."

"Thanks, Shon. I appreciate your honesty." Whitney's other line beeped. "Look, that's Chench. Let me answer this. See you in a few days, B to the FF."

"Looking forward to it," Shon confirmed.

Whitney ended her call and accepted Chench's. She barely listened to him as all she could think about was that in less than seventy-two hours, she and Shon would be boarding a plane for a much needed getaway.

Chapter Thirty-Three

The captain had just announced that they were about to descend. The seatbelt indicator beeped, signaling for all passengers to strap up for landing. Once the plane touched down safely, Whitney helped Shon with the kids. They grabbed their luggage and exited the airport, headed for the private transportation Whitney's sponsor had secured.

"Bitch! How the hell do you manage to do the shit you do?" Shon asked excitedly.

"I do things that others won't, so I can benefit from what others don't." Whitney smirked and winked at Shon.

"You're a whole hot mess, you know that?" Shon adjusted a sleeping Quazier on her lap and checked to make sure her phone was on.

"Expecting a call?" Whitney asked.

"Yeah, their dad has a parole hearing today. He's supposed to be calling me. I pray he's coming home soon. I need help with these kids," Shon admitted.

Although Whitney didn't show it, the thought of Shon finally getting her family back together only reminded her of how lonely her personal life was. As of late, she had been secretly wondering if she was partially to blame for her own bleakness. A family *sounded* nice, it was just something Whitney wasn't ready for at the time but second guessed it. However, now wasn't the time for that, she was ready for a good time.

"We're going to have so much fun! I hired the best damn nanny in all of Dade County," Whitney cheered.

"Girl, I sure hope so. I am not feeling having my kids around a random-ass stranger. I know we met her through Skype, but people put up a good front."

"Shon, haven't I proved my worthiness by now? I had three different background checks run on her, at least twenty different reference checks, and damn near obtained a blood sample. She's legit-legit, okay? Her resume is squeaky. Plus, I read in her bio that she nannied for Eddie Murphy's ex-wife and even Kris Jenner back in the day. I can't see anybody trying to ruin all that good money with a bad reputation."

"Well, damn! I don't think you told me *all* that!"

They arrived at the beachfront condo in North Beach, Miami and unpacked. Shortly after they got settled, the middle-aged Italian nanny showed up, prepared to assist. For the first night, Whitney was able to convince Shon to take a hands-off approach with the kids and simply observe, stepping in to make suggestions when necessary so she could witness whether the nanny met her expectations. Just as Whitney expected, she did. The nanny was patient, gentle, and hands-on with the kids. They began to take to her better than Shon expected. Shon was so comfortable with the nanny that she practically talked Whitney into stepping out the same night, so she could take in the sights of a place she had never been.

They bar hopped, walked the strip, and engaged in conversation with whomever they so pleased.

"Bones, did you see his ass? Damn, Quavier better hurry up home. I am in heat, literally and sexually, fo sho!"

"I can't believe you went this long with no sex. I mean if you're feeling kinky, act on it! You never did anything since he's been gone?"

"Nope. I thought about it a few times, though, but I would feel so bad cheating on him."

"He never cheated on you?" Whitney was all about reciprocity.

Shon's lack of response was the answer she needed.

"Okay, so look at it like this, you are not cheating on him; you are fulfilling a need. If your kids needed diapers or formula and the only way to provide that was to sleep with a man, would you?"

"Yes, of course. I'd do anything for my kids."

"So, you wouldn't do anything for yourself? C'mon, Shon, we only get one life, and if there's something you want, even if for a moment, why deprive yourself of that? It's not like you're leaving him for good or to fend for himself. From what I've noticed, you are a damn good woman to him and an amazing mom to the kids. If you have an unmet need that he created, why not do something that's going to make you feel good? That's all I'm saying. But what do I know? I've been selfish all my life, and I rarely, if ever, put anyone above me," Whitney confessed.

"Yeah, we'll see. The vacation is still young, and there seems to be a litany of options in this part of the country," Shon said sheepishly.

~ ~ ~

Whitney met Lina and Simone in the parking lot of the private residence, which was rented by one of Whitney's most generous sponsors, Dr. Blakemore. After sampling Whitney at her mother's fundraising event, he had been contacting her regularly to fulfill his guilty pleasures. Now, as he and two of his frat brothers were about to fulfill a friendship pact to tie the knot on the same night, he wanted his final hoorah as a single man to be one they'd never forget. Whitney made sure he'd hired Lina's Whiskey on Wheels business as the private bartending service and Simone's Sensual Massages for relaxation. Just like that, she had secured checks and tax-free tips for herself and two of her friends.

While Lina offered body shots from the most sacred areas of her being and Simone gave happy endings, Whitney had a private room so she could do what she did best: fulfill fantasies for those with wild fetishes. When she walked away

Dr. Blakemore and another man followed her, letting her know it was time to start the party.

"Two for one tonight, fellas?"

"We were hoping we could cuckold?" Blakemore's buddy asked.

"I can do anything, but that's such an amateur request. I'm sure you have deeper fantasies than that."

Blakemore and company looked at each other and turned back to Whitney.

"You sure anything goes? And you won't be uncomfortable or freaked out?" Dr. Blakemore asked.

She looked at them both and smiled. "As long as it doesn't involve babies, animals, and old people, I promise you, we'll have a grand time."

Blakemore walked over to a duffel bag located in the corner of the room, opened it and pulled out a strap on. "Is this acceptable?"

Whitney grinned harder. "My kind of party, gentleman."

For hours on end, they partied in more ways than one, and by the end of the event, Whitney was twenty grand richer than when she had arrived. That's why she was grateful when Shon and the nanny decided to take the kids outside to the beach for a walk. Her body had needed the rest and her mind the quietness. By the time they returned, she was ready for what the night had to offer.

"Look who's up and at 'em!" Shon joked when she saw Whitney walking from the bathroom, wiping her mouth and holding her stomach.

"I think I drank way too much last night."

"Or you could be pregnant. Ever think of that?"

"I doubt that. I use protection."

"So, you telling me Chench never let one off in you?" Shon asked skeptically.

"Once, twice at most, and that's because we were high and not thinking, but that was a couple of months back."

"Whelp, those are accurate calculations. You usually start to see signs around this time."

Whitney didn't want to engage in that type of talk or even think about what Shon was suggesting. In two days, they'd be heading home, and she was looking forward to enjoying the rest of her time in Miami. "Enough of that nonsense. I have something for you."

"Okay, let me bring this bottle to Quaz. The nanny is laying them down for a nap. Meet you back here."

Whitney went to her room and retrieved her folder. She'd been waiting months to deliver the news to Shon and felt good knowing that she could even make such a proposal. When Shon reentered the room, Whitney asked her to sit.

"I know you've been looking for a full-time job, but I wanted to propose something to you first." Whitney slid the manila envelope over to Shon and told her to open it. "That's all the paperwork for a new nonprofit I just started called RJG Foundation. I designed it to be a legal advocacy agency, where people in the LGBTQ community can seek information and get connected to resources for wills, powers of attorney, health care proxies, etc. We won't provide legal representation, per se, but we will draft documents on their behalf, make phone calls, and send legal letters if needed. Everything is outlined in the bylaws and supporting documentation." Whitney watched as Shon scanned the paperwork. Her expression went from perplexed to awe.

"RJG, as in Rohan Jackson Garland?" Shon asked for clarity.

Whitney nodded. "I need an executive director, someone to oversee the day-to-day operations and plan and organize *official* fundraisers," she said with a smile. "And coordinate the needs of the office, whatever that may entail. The budget, right now, is thirty-five thousand a year, which comes out to about seven hundred a week or twenty dollars an hour. With some dedication and creativity, I'm sure we can increase it over time. There's enough money to cover the first year's salary, and I'm hoping you'll accept the position."

Shon looked at the documents and slowly raised her eyes to meet Whitney's. At that moment, Whitney realized she enjoyed what it felt like to be unselfish, to give something to someone with no strings attached, truly from the heart. In the short time she had come to know Jackson, he had impacted her life more than she could ever give him credit for. He showed her what genuine friendship was all about and never judged her for her indiscretions. Now, as she entered a deeper friendship with his twin sister, she couldn't think of a better way to honor her first B to the FF while supporting her current one.

"Wow, I don't think anyone has ever done something so charitable for me, let alone my brother. Like, Bones, I don't think you know how honored I am that you did all this and even thought enough of me to put me in such a position." Shon got emotional. "I've never run a business before."

"As long as our hearts are in the right place, we'll be fine. Plus, I have all the players in place to help us be successful. We have a great, diverse board of directors. I recruited some folks I met while working at the LGBTQ center and secured a knowledgeable accountant. Only thing you have to do is keep the mission alive and maintain the vision."

Shon walked around the table and gave Whitney the biggest hug. "I love you, Whitney. Thank you so much!"

Whitney didn't say she loved her back, but deep in her heart, whatever she was feeling had to be comparable. "Come on, girl. You know I'm not good with all this sentimental nonsense. I presented, you accepted, we're good!"

Shon laughed and wiped her eyes. "One day, that ice is going to melt from your heart and you're going to be the happiest you've ever been. Watch!"

If Shon thought that was the only surprise on the trip then she was wrong. Whitney had found out that Memphis Bleek and a few other Roc-a-Fella artists were performing at the local nightclub, and she couldn't wait to see her friend's reaction when she found out they had backstage passes. Whitney didn't feel a need to embrace her father's other child. In her mind, Shon was the sister she never had and, as far as she was concerned, the only one she'd ever need.

Chapter Thirty-Four

When Whitney returned from her trip, the only thing she wanted to do was rest and relax. She didn't even have the energy to unpack, so she placed the suitcase in the corner of her bedroom, where it stayed for two days. She had been feeling very tired lately and had no desire to do anything, but eat and sleep, so when Chench called, she wished she hadn't answered the phone.

"Yo, get down here now!" Chench ordered. "Homeboy is here, and I need you to find out what he's up to, how he's moving, and who he's movin' with."

Whitney reluctantly hopped into the shower and picked out her favorite go-to jeans and a cleavage-revealing blouse. She ended up having to change when she noticed how snug her jeans were fitting. *I need to hit the gym,* she told herself.

As soon as she walked into the bar, Chench walked over to her.

"That's him, right there, talking to those three dudes. He's the one wearing the black polo and gray jeans. Be casual but persistent. Make sure you take his drink orders and be very friendly. If you get him to hang around, then you got him."

"And what exactly do you want to know? Just where he works, lives, and who his friends are?" Whitney was still confused about the whole thing and thought it was rather silly.

Chench sucked his teeth and sighed. "I need to know as much shit as you can get me. I think the mufucka is runnin' back telling people shit about how my boys operate, and it's causing us unnecessary attention from the law. They think he's A-one but I feel different. So use your magic and see if you can get him to reveal anything, aiight?"

And I think you're being paranoid. Whitney yawned. "Yeah, okay."

"Damn, what's wrong with you? You seem sluggish as hell." Chench dug into his pocket. "Here, go take a hit or something. Perk your ass up." He handed her a small bundle.

Although Whitney had been laying off the coke and scotch, she admitted that she did need a pick up. She took the contents from Chench and walked into the bathroom. When she walked out, she felt much more energetic than she had when she'd entered. She also felt a little nauseous. When she got to the bar, she poured herself some ginger ale and sipped that while scanning the crowd. When she spotted her target and his friends, she walked over to them before the other bartender could.

"Hello, what can I get you?" She said to the guy wearing the black polo.

He flashed her a smile. “I need three shots of Henny, two Heinekens, and a Long Island, please.”

Damn, he’s cute and has manners. Whitney shared her signature smile. “Coming right up.”

All night, he returned to her for his alcoholic requests and she served him with the best service. She watched as he consumed beverage after beverage with his friends and each time she tried to initiate conversation, the guy brushed her off. She looked over at Chench and he jerked his head, encouraging her to persist. Whitney was growing frustrated. It was late, she was tired—mainly of Chench— and just wanted to be home in her bed, but she also had to admit that the coke had her feeling horny. The ruckus from the crew she had just been serving caught her attention. The guy in the black polo and gray jeans was now lying on the floor.

“I told you not to give him another drink. He was done before we got here.” One of the guys who was with him said.

“He’s grown and said he could handle it.” Another guy chimed in.

“Man, let’s get the fuck outta here. This shit’s embarrassing.”

The two men picked their friend up off the floor and carried him out. As soon as they walked away, Chench walked over to her.

“What the fuck was so hard about what I asked?” He was visibly upset.

"It wasn't hard, I just didn't have a chance to." Whitney shot back. "Clearly he couldn't hold his liquor. That's not my fault."

"And clearly you couldn't do what I asked."

"I can come down here again, Chench. It's not that big of a deal."

"Nah, fuck it. It's a wrap. This was the perfect set up and you fucked it up. I'll look into this shit myself." He said and walked away.

Whitney was upset and felt humiliated. She truly believed he was paranoid and that his getting arrested had nothing to do with this guy. She was about to pack her shit and get the hell out of there when a man approached her for a drink.

"Hey, what can I get you? Whitney inquired.

"Some of your time." The attractive man stated.

Whitney smirked. She needed a release and this stranger was right on time. "I'm Jasmine," she said, offering up her alias.

"Tristan. Nice to meet you," he replied.

Whitney spent the next two hours serving up drinks to Tristan and his crew. At two in the morning, the deejay announced, "Last call for alcohol," and by two thirty, they were cleaning the bar. At three a.m. Tristan was in the car with Whitney as he guided her to a nearby hotel. He said he and his boys had some money to spend and he was hoping to do it with her. With the opportunity to acquire some extra cash and experience a new type of sponsor, Whitney didn't object. Based on the two-hundred-dollar tip she'd made from them alone, she knew the rest of the night would be good, except it wasn't. Her plan to secure new sponsors backfired leaving her feeling mortified.

The night had gone worse than she'd expected and all she wanted to do was place her head under a pillow and stay there. When she pulled into her driveway and saw that Chench's car was parked in front of her house, she rolled her eyes. *Please don't let this man be in a pissy mood.* The calls he had placed to her went unanswered as she refused to talk to him after the way he treated her at the bar. Before going straight home, she stopped at the drug store and made a necessary purchase. She walked into the house and went straight to her bedroom where he was sound asleep, grateful for the peace. She took off her clothes, used the bathroom, showered, and did her best to rid her mind of what had taken place moments ago. After moistening her skin, she slid in bed on her side and was fast asleep within minutes.

It felt like her eyes had only been closed a few seconds, when she heard the shower running. Whitney looked over at her clock and saw that it wasn't on, reasoning that Chench must have unplugged it to charge his cell. Curious as to what time it was, she picked up his phone and noticed that it was unlocked. Just as she registered the time, a text message came through. It was from Chaianne. She wouldn't normally look through his phone or question his whereabouts, but she quickly concluded that this time was warranted. She opened the message, hoping to see a long thread of communication, but was immediately disappointed.

Chaianne: What time should I be ready, Dominic?

Chench: By noon

Chaianne: Okay

Ready? For what? Where are they going? Those questions prompted Whitney to dig further. She opened a thread between him and his friend, Rob. Although the message history was short as well, it answered her questions.

Rob: Aiight bro, be safe and enjoy. Who you rolling with to the boxing match?

Chench: Chai coming with me. She had a situation recently, so I invited her to get her out of town for the weekend.

Rob: That's what's up. Y'all have a good time. Treat her right, man. She's always been my favorite.

Chench: Mine too. AC is the perfect drive to convince her I'm the best man for her.

Rob: You's a funny nigga. Good luck with that. I doubt she want ya ass back after all that.

Whitney was hurt, upset, betrayed, and even more curious about Chaianne and Chench than she was before. She wondered why, if they were broken up and Chaianne was with someone else, would she even agree to go out of town with him. *Has he been lying to me all this time?* He could've used Chaianne's investigative skills to carry out his paranoid dirty work, Whitney reasoned. When she heard the shower turn off she quickly closed out the message window, placed his phone back where it was, and rolled over, acting like she was still resting. As she lay in bed, contemplating how to broach the situation with Chench, he exited the bathroom, holding something she wished she could make disappear. *Shit!*

"Got something you want to share?" he asked, holding up the pregnancy test she had discarded.

"Huh?" she said, feigning ignorance. She lifted her head from her pillow to see what was in his hand. "Oh, no, that's Shon's," she lied. No need in being honest about something that would never come to fruition.

"Shon's, huh? Ain't her man locked up?" Chench stared at her and watched her discomfort.

"Uh, yeah. Yes, he is. But that doesn't mean anything." Whitney got up and walked into the bathroom.

"So, you just gonna kill our baby?" he asked as he followed her. "Or should I be asking if it's even mine. Your phone's busier than a dope boy's and you didn't even bother to come home last night."

Whitney gave him a face that let him know he was being ridiculous. She wasn't big on lying so she decided to be honest with him. She ignored the coming home comment and addressed what she saw as the bigger issue. “Look, I’m not ready for all that comes with being a mother.” *I don’t think I ever will be*. “I enjoy life just the way it is right now. I don’t have time for a child.” She avoided eye contact with him.

Chench walked over to her and grabbed her around the waist. “Don’t do this to me, to *us*. This baby will be what we need to complete us.”

“Complete us? We’ve only been seeing each other for a little over a year now, and at no time were we exclusive. We’re not engaged or married, so how would a whole human being complete us?” She wondered why she was even debating this with him.

“Is that what you want, a ring? I can make that happen,” he offered. The truth was Chench had wanted a child for a while now. He’d even begged Chaianne to stop taking her birth control, but to no avail.

Whitney witnessed the sincerity in his eyes and even though she felt like crap, she couldn’t allow that to sway her. “The only thing I want is my career and my freedom.”

Chench was taken aback. “The only thing? What the fuck am I?”

“You know what I meant.”

“No, I don’t but I do know what you said. I can’t believe this shit.” He started getting dressed. “You just like the rest of them bitches. Just want what *you* want and fuck everyone else."

"The rest? I'm sorry, but I'm definitely not like the rest. But you, my friend, are no different than any other condescending, misogynistic, cheating-ass man. When were you going to tell me you were still sniffing the crotch of your ex-bitch!?"

"What ex, Chai? Man, that ain't nothing. She don't want me. She let somebody else get her wide open."

"Ah, so you're jealous."

"Hell no!"

"Still love her?"

"Hell no!"

"Lies! Lies, lies, lies. And if there's one of many things I despise, it's a liar." Whitney finished putting on her clothes and walked out of the room and away from Chench. His lack of admission to still being in love with her nemesis bothered her more than she cared to admit. The fact that she was competing with Chaianne on two fronts was tough and only confirmed just how deep it bothered her to know that the two men she cared about the most, loved the same woman she hated just as much.

Fuck her, fuck him, and fuck them! Whitney stormed out of the house, slamming her front door on the way. She didn't feel a twinge of guilt when she dialed the number to Planned

Parenthood in the next town over to make an appointment to abort a child she knew for a fact was his.

Chapter Thirty-Five

Making it through the work week was tough. As much as Whitney tried to do her best to not think about Chench and where he was or what he was doing, she still found herself distracted with thoughts of him. A part of her was feeling extremely guilty for terminating the pregnancy just two days before. Today would have been his court appearance, but, as promised, she'd made arrangements with Yiellow in exchange for Chench's get out of jail free card. After their "meeting," Yiellow reported to his boss that his breathalyzer had malfunctioned the night of Chench's arrest, which led to inaccurate readings, so they had no choice but to drop the charges when he showed up. It had been five days since she'd last seen or heard from him, and she wished she could just erase him from her mind and her ... *Nah, this can't be what I think it is*, she pondered. She had never felt this strange when missing someone, or this hurt due to a breakup, but she wasn't completely convinced that what she was feeling was love.

Grateful that it was Therapy Thursday, Whitney left work and headed straight to her appointment. When she walked in, Dr. Keptin wasted no time picking up where they'd left off. She had asked Whitney a question and sat patiently as she allowed the long pause and uncomfortable silence to propel Whitney to answer. As a professional, she was trained to sit through awkward stillness, and give her client the time and space to formulate a well-thought-out response.

"To be honest, I don't know why I can't embrace her. There's nothing in me that desires to do so. It's almost like I'd be forcing myself to accept something I'm totally at peace with rejecting."

"You don't think that takes a lot of energy?"

Whitney shrugged. "Not really."

"So, let me get this straight. You have wiped your mother from your life, there's now a disconnect with your father, you refuse to welcome your sister, you won't acknowledge the hurt you've caused Patrick, and you haven't told your current lover that he was a pawn in your chess game. However, you have taken in your deceased best friend's sister, holding her close, and honoring his name. You're showing that you are, in fact, capable of love. You're just being selective about who you choose to share it with. Tell me about that. Why them?"

"I've thought about that, and Jackson was the first person who made me feel comfortable in my own skin. He seemed to genuinely accept me for who I am and not what I had. It was almost like he saw my greatness and value despite my habits and flaws. That was new for me. In a way, Jackson instilled confidence in me that I hadn't secured for myself. I began to relish in the authentic me because of him. Then when he died, having Shon was like having a female replica of Jackson. So, to answer your question, I say why not them?"

Dr. Keptin nodded. "I see. Let me kick this back to you. Have you exposed the real you to the others and allowed them to witness that side of your greatness?"

"My parents should see it. They know me the best."

"No, I don't think they know you at all. From what we've discussed, I don't think you've given your mom the chance to get to know you. Your disdain for her has blocked your willingness to open up to her. Your father has always been too much of a go-getter to actually try and learn you. It seems like he corrected your tantrums with gifts, your sassiness with threats, and your demands with agreeance. You recruited Chench so you could spy on your sister without having to do the real work of interacting with her. Are you ever going to tell him the truth?"

"No, I don't think he needs to know anything more than what he already does. This arrangement is just as much a benefit to him as it is to me."

"And how is that?" Dr. Keptin inquired.

"I'm helping him become a legitimate businessman, and he's helping me become ... better!"

"Better how? What has he helped you with?"

"For starters, he embraces my natural beauty. He always tells me how beautiful and sexy I am. He loves having me around, doesn't mind showing me off to his friends, and relishes in my presence when we're in public. He's the first man that I am completely attracted to who has shown me just how much he cares and loves me."

"Do you love him?"

Something about the way the question rolled off Dr. Keptin's tongue let Whitney know it wasn't your average question about loving a man.

"I'm not sure I know what that feels like." Whitney was one hundred percent honest. She failed to share the sentiments Chench so freely spoke of because she wasn't sure if what she felt was love.

"I see." Dr. Keptin nodded. "I'm going to ask you some questions that only you can answer honestly. If your answer to these questions is 'yes,' then young lady, you're in love."

Whitney straightened her back, cleared her mind, and readied herself to receive the questions in a way that would allow her to be truthful about the answers. When Dr. Keptin asked if she was ready, she nodded.

"Okay, here it is. And you don't have to answer out loud if you don't want." She offered Whitey a soft smile. "Did your interest in him increase over time? Are you just as—if not more—attracted to him now than you were on the first night? Has he done things that would normally turn you off, but instead, cause you to turn a blind eye? Do you find that you want him around more often than not? Is he on your mind when you wake up, throughout the day, and when you go to bed? Are you often checking on his wellbeing and wondering if he's safe? Have you done things with and for him that you haven't done for others? Does this man make you second guess decisions you knew you were sure about prior to meeting him, causing you to now give them more thought? Do you find yourself not wanting to disappoint him for fear of losing him?" Dr. Keptin paused for a second and looked straight into Whitney's eyes. "If you answered yes to all of those questions or most, it's safe to say your heart has found a mate."

Whitney sat up straighter and looked at the clock. She picked up her handbag from the floor and placed it on her lap to retrieve the copay. "Wow, look at the time."

"Like I said, you don't have to admit it to me but be honest with yourself. My challenge to you is if you do love this man, consider telling him the truth, the whole truth, and nothing but the truth. No real relationship can be sustained if the foundation was built on lies."

Whitney handed Dr. Keptin a twenty-dollar bill and stood up. "Thank you. You can text me the confirmation for our next appointment."

Chapter Thirty-Six

On her way home, Whitney's cellphone vibrated. She searched for it in her purse as she navigated traffic. Deep inside, she prayed and hoped it was Chench. Normally, she would have called him several times by now but the truth was she was hurt, too. Just when she'd admitted that she cared, he'd wiped his ass on her heart and didn't seem the least bit bothered. When she saw it was her dad, she reluctantly answered.

"Hi, Daddy."

"Hey, baby. Is something wrong? I thought we agreed to meet today? At least that's what's on my calendar."

"Oh, shoot. I'm sorry. I totally forgot about that. What do you want to talk to me about?"

"That bomb I dropped on you about having a sister. I want to give you the opportunity to ask whatever questions you may have, and I will be totally honest. I rented a suite for the night, so we can meet here and talk freely."

Whitney was over the whole ordeal with her dad. Yes, she had questions, and no, she surely didn't want more lies, but she wasn't sure if she was up for the raw truth either.

“I had a long week, Daddy. To be honest, I’m mentally and emotionally drained. I don’t think I’m in the mood for anything that’s going to upset or agitate me.”

“Skittles, my intent isn’t to do either. If you don’t want to come to me, I can come to your place. How’s that?”

Whitney gave his offer some thought. Maybe this talk with her dad was what she needed.” Okay, sure. Come by in an hour.

When she got home, she did a brief but thorough job of straightening up. She washed dishes, fluffed cushions and pillows, and vacuumed the floors. She and Chench had been having so much sex that she worried the scent would seep from the walls. The last thing she did before showering and getting dressed was light some candles.

When her father arrived, Whitney had two bottles of water on her coffee table and offered him one when they sat.

“Let me get right to it,” Frederick began. “When I got wind of the pregnancy, I approached her mom, Trinda, and she told me the baby wasn’t mine and it belonged to another man. She had no reason to lie, so I left it alone. Weeks before you entered the world, the topic resurfaced again. Aunt Val was friends with a woman who worked with Trinda, and the woman told her that I may have fathered the child. I had Valene’s friend give my information to Trinda but she never reached out to me. Two years later, Valene ran into Trinda and the baby. When she saw her, she was convinced that the baby was my child. Valene told Pa and Ma, and they called me asking about it. By that time, I had already transferred out of state to go to law school and was busy with classes. Valene got Trinda to agree to a paternity test, and it came back proving that the baby was mine." Frederick took a sip of water and continued. "Pa and Ma took on the responsibility of reaching out to Trinda to try and have a relationship with their grandchild, but the letters went unanswered and the calls unreturned. We later found out they moved around a lot because Trinda struggled financially, so they never really had any stability. When it came to telling you about your sister, I honestly didn't know when the right time was. I feared if I told you, you would tell your mom and I couldn't risk that. At that time we were already married, she and I were going through our issues, and she was looking for anything and everything she could to discredit me as a husband and disgrace me as a man. I wanted to tell you when you graduated high school, but I wasn't sure of the effect it would have and didn't want to ruin your college experience. I didn't tell you when you finished undergrad because you were so excited and focused on entering law school." Frederick looked at Whitney, who was sitting on the other couch, listening quietly. "To be honest, I never knew when the right time was or should be. So when I knew you were practically all done with law school, I figured that was the best time, and I am so so sorry I waited that long. Your sister's name is Chaianne Lewis, and she was born on

March 22nd, six months before you. Yes, I was aware she had been in foster care, before going into a group home, and that she had a daughter and was looking for a house."

"If you didn't have contact with her, how were you aware of all that she was going through?" Whitney asked.

"Well, we knew about the lack of stability when Pa went by the address she'd listed on the paternity test and was told by the landlord that she had been evicted months prior. The landlord told him to check with someone else and when he went to that house, they told Pa that she had been kicked out and was staying at another location. Needless to say, every place he looked into led to dead ends. Ma tried mailing letters with checks and gifts, but they always came back as undeliverable and now we know why."

"How did you find out about foster care?"

"I began to make connections. I had a friend from law school who became a family law attorney. He used his connections and linked me with the right people. That's how I found out that Trinda was arrested for selling prescription drugs and Chaianne had been placed in foster care. I reached out to the social workers about getting custody. They were willing to allow Chaianne to be with family, except by the time we showed interest, Chaianne had expressed disinterest in meeting anyone. She only wanted her mom and was very fearful of meeting someone new. I guess she'd had a bad experience with foster parents. Eventually, the social worker and law guardian felt it was in her best interest to leave her be, but they were kind enough to keep me updated."

"How old is her daughter? And who told you she had a baby?"

"I believe she's six years old now. By the time she gave birth, Chaianne had aged out of the group home and was living with the daughter's paternal grandmother before securing a place of her own. I did my part by secretly paying some of her monthly bills, enough to help out but not too much to make her suspicious. I sent money toward her tuition so the amount she had to take out for loans was minimal."

"And Nana and Pa's house?" That was Whitney's biggest question. "How did it come to be hers? Was that your plan all along and if so, why even offer it to me?"

"No, no, of course not. When I called you about the house, I wanted it to be yours. I would have quietly helped Chaianne with something else. But when you were adamant about not wanting it, she came to mind. I kept tabs on her by using my clout to communicate with those whom she interacted with such as her school counselors, the housing authority, and her realtor. When I found out she was looking for a house, I took Ma and Pa's off the market, lowered the price so it was in her price range, and allowed her to do a rent-to-own agreement so she didn't have to take out a mortgage. The money she pays will go into a trust fund for her daughter."

Whitney rubbed her chest and patted her neck. She had no idea her father was this involved. It actually impressed her and made her sad. She knew he had done just as much for her if not more, but the fact that she had to hear how much work and energy he'd put into a child he never met was a little unsettling.

"Do you love her? I mean are your feelings for her the same as you have for me?"

Now, it was Frederick's turn to rub and pat. "I have pondered that question, and I can honestly say that, yes, I do love Chaianne. I'm unable to compare you two because I was there when you were born, I held you in my arms, I shared in many of your firsts, I celebrated birthdays with you. I've wiped your tears when you were sad, eased your pain when you were hurt, and did everything in my power to make you happy. I didn't have any of that with her and it makes me sad. I feel bad about the way things transpired; however, I can't change the past. The only thing I can do is move forward, and that's why I'm doing everything in my power to take the steps necessary to bring her into our lives."

"Why now, though? Why not just continue being her savior in the shadows and wait for her to seek you out?"

"I've thought about just reaching out to her but to be honest, Skittles, I'm a little afraid and apprehensive. I'm not sure what her mother has shared with her or how she would receive me. I guess I have a hard time exposing my vulnerabilities to the women in my life for fear of being hurt or hurting them. I feel like it's my responsibility to extend my hand. She's my child. The onus is on me to make it right, and that's what I plan to do." Frederick got up and sat next to Whitney. "I need you to help me with this. Since Ma has gotten worse, it really opened my eyes to how short life is and even if we get the quantity in years, the quality is unpredictable. Chaianne has a right to know and meet her family. I'm just afraid to make the move... alone. You wouldn't know this, but she started her own private investigation business and recently took on a cheating spouse case. As life would have it, the cheating husband happens to be your aunt Valene's crazy ex, that guy Mitch. Come to find out, he was so adamant about not losing his wife to divorce and paying a large alimony that he held his wife hostage and hired someone to kill your sister."

Holy shit! "Kill her? She's dead?!" *Fuck! I knew Mitch was crazy but not that crazy. I expected him to do something just not to that extreme*. Rub, pat. Repeat.

"No. Whoever this guy was that Mitch hired must have backed out, so Mitch found out where she lived and went to do the work himself. Thank God her daughter's dad showed up when he did or she would be." Frederick lowered his head in shame.

Whitney didn't like Chaianne but she didn't want her dead. "That's crazy," she stated.

"Tell me about it. The police chief and I play golf together. He knew about Chaianne, and as soon as he got wind of the situation, he notified me immediately. That's how I got all this information."

"So, Mitch is caught? Off the streets?"

"Oh, yeah. He's behind bars as we speak and will be for a very, very long time. They found his wife hidden in their home behind a wall. She was alive when they located her but she was in bad shape."

"That man is really crazy, then!" Whitney couldn't believe what she was hearing.

"Yeah, we knew that way back then. I'm just glad Valene got away from him and pursued that order of protection. Lord knows what could have happened if she didn't."

"So, everything is good, you know, with her and the little girl?" Whitney wasn't sure if she was asking out of concern or curiosity, but it was a question she wanted answered.

"Yes, they are both doing well. I had alarms installed at the house and she was pleased with the added safety feature. The police chief also agreed to have someone detail her neighborhood for a while, just in case the hired killer returned."

"I can't believe I'm about to say this but I'm proud of you, Daddy. Even though I gave you a hard time about it in the beginning, knowing how you are as a father, if I was her, I'd appreciate all your efforts. I think you should reach out to her."

"So, are you saying you want to meet her, too?"

Whitney chuckled. "No, I'm not saying that at all. I can't say I won't ever come around to it but, right now, I'm not ready."

Frederick nodded slowly, not in agreement but understanding. "Although I was hoping for a different answer, I will respect your decision and pray that you'll come around sooner, than later." Frederick stood and grabbed Whitney's hand so she could stand, too. "Thank you, Skittles. I can't tell you how much I appreciate you for allowing me to get this off my chest. My shoulders feel lighter and my heart less troubled. I love you more than anything in this world."

"Don't say anything because, clearly, you have to share your heart."

"Skittles, you've been sharing my heart for the last twenty-plus years and didn't even know it. That should be all the confirmation you need to know that despite me having another child, it never interfered with the magnitude of my love for you."

Whitney thought about his statement for the rest of the night. It was liberating and stifling. On one hand, she realized the truth of his words and gathered that all this time, him having another daughter, never once interfered with their relationship. On the other, had she realized that when he'd first revealed his secret, she may not have reacted the way she did or done the things she'd done for revenge.

Whitney went to bed that night with a lot on her mind, but nothing compared to the heaviness she would feel from a call the following morning.

Chapter Thirty-Seven

Back-to-back court cases guaranteed that Whitney was going to have a busy day, so when she saw Shon's seven missed calls and a text message: "Call me back ASAP! It's important," she couldn't even find the time to respond until she was back at her office. She reasoned that she would wait until she got off the elevator and behind a closed door to call her friend. Something inside her didn't feel right, though. A young guy on the elevator kept staring at her and smirking. When she got off, she saw two of her female colleagues standing in the breakroom, whispering, and when she walked by them, they didn't even say hello, as they threw their noses in the air.

She closed her door and called Shon.

"Bones, I don't even know how to tell you this," Shon began.

"What, what is it, Shon? Just say it."

"You're on the Internet. Those three guys you linked up with at that bar posted a video of you giving them head and your reaction when you found out they were recording you."

Whitney wasn't surprised about the video but she was shocked that they'd aired it. She hadn't told Shon or anyone what happened that night she'd hooked up with Tristan. She just hoped they'd keep it to themselves for laughs and giggles. She had been recorded before by past sponsors, but they never disgraced her in public and she never thought they'd do it, either. The past trauma Jason had inflicted back in middle school and the hate she felt for him and all the boys who looked like him came racing back to her in a major way.

"Whitney? You still there?" Shon called out. "I'm so sorry they did this. I will get to the bottom of it and make sure they remove it."

"I, I gotta go, Shon." Whitney didn't wait for a response.

She hung up, gathered her personal items, and left work. She called out the next day and the day after that. During the entire drive home, she tried to reach Chench. She contemplated leaving him a message when he didn't answer, but she wasn't sure what she would say. "Did you see the video? I'm sorry for not coming home that night because if I did none of this would have happened. Please forgive me for killing your, well our baby. MoneyWorx wasn't to help you; it was to get back at your ex-girlfriend, Chaianne, who by the way happens to be my sister." She may not have been ready to admit her wrongs, but she needed an outlet to vent her frustrations and decided to instead call him out on his. When she heard the beep, she began her rant. "You piece of shit! You're still fucking that bitch and instead of being honest you lied! How the fuck could you do that to me? To *me,* of all people? I fucking cared about you, put my good sense aside to help you, and that's how you treat me? Why, Chench, huh? Why? I'm so glad I got rid of that fucking baby. I'd never want to share a child with a slime ball like you. I hope the rest of your life is miserable. I hate you and never want to see you again!" Whitney screamed as tears and spittle speckled her face. She ended the message and threw her phone at the dashboard. She drove home in a daze, with little to no interest in anything or anyone.

Hours felt like days and days felt like weeks. When Monday came, Whitney concluded that she was in no shape to go to work that day or any other day that week. The five days off consisted of her favorite vices and they had taken a toll on her body. She was grateful that she was no longer harboring an invader inside her belly. She had a new deadbolt installed so Chench wouldn't be able to use his key. Calls, texts, and random knocks at her door weren't enough to get her out of bed. But when the cops threatened to break down the door, she knew she had to get up and answer it.

Whitney cracked the door with the chain still attached.

"Ma'am, we're here for a safety check. Your friends and family haven't heard from you and asked us to come by."

"I'm fine. You can go away now," she mumbled as she tried to close the door.

"Whitney, it's me. Can I please come in?" Shon was standing next to the officer, wearing a look of pure concern on her face.

"Not right now. Maybe later." Whitney tried closing the door on them but Shon's foot stopped it.

"No, I think now is better. Please." She turned to the officer and whispered that she had it from there. Once he was reassured that everything was fine, he turned to leave. When he walked away, Shon pleaded with Whitney to let her in.

Whitney closed the door and removed the latch to let Shon enter. She was immediately taken aback by the condition of her friend's home. Whitney was one of the neatest and most organized people she knew but her condo looked as if it had been occupied by drunk college students. Takeout containers were all over the place. Used napkins lay on the floor. Dishes were piled in the sink, and the garbage was overflowing. But Shon never said anything as she placed her things on the kitchen island.

She went into the bathroom and ran some bathwater for her friend. She walked inside the room and helped Whitney undress. She didn't ask any questions or make any statements. Once Whitney was undressed, Shon walked her into the bathroom and waited until she was situated inside the tub. She turned on the jets and left Whitney to relax while she tended to the rest of the house.

Shon returned to the bathroom and washed Whitney's back, legs, and feet and shampooed her hair. She lathered the rag and instructed her to wash her private areas. When Whitney was all done, Shon drained the tub and wrapped a towel around her when she got out. When they entered the living room, Whitney looked around and took note of how clean the place was. She inhaled the scent of the lit candles.

The empty whiskey bottle and small mound of coke on the nightstand told Shon most of what she needed to know. Her friend was self-medicating to mask her pain.

"My life is ruined, Shon. I can't go back to work after this. Why would he do that to me?"

Shon watched as her strong, fearless, confident friend displayed a level of vulnerability she had never seen. She rubbed Whitney's back to comfort her. "I don't know what would possess Tristan to do some shit like this. He's always been a super cool guy and this seems so out of character for him."

"I'm not talking about Tristan. I mean Chench. If he hadn't mistreated me at the bar that night I never would have even left with Tristan. And then to come home and find out that he's still sleeping with Chaianne was the ultimate betrayal." Whitney wiped a tear from her eye and then her nose. "I really felt like we would work. I wanted it to work for us. I was so into him. He probably sent Tristan to me so he could do his thing with Chaianne. I feel set up."

Shon's face went from empathetic to perplexed. "Wait, I'm confused. From what I was told, Chench had nothing to do with this."

"I'm sure he did. The timing was too perfect. He practically rushed me out the house to go down to the bar to extract information from this random ass dude, who he thinks is behind he and his friends increased police contact, then the guy gets drunk and leaves, Chench gets upset with me and then here comes Tristan and his friends. I should have known better, being high and horny erased my common sense."

"Whit, that may be a possibility, but I don't think that's what happened. According to Vera, word on the street is that Chaianne talked Tristan into doing that as a form of get back for you trying to talk to her man down at the bar and for all those other run-ins y'all had because of Chench. She told him you worked down there and he could find you there on the weekends. Chaianne is best friend's with Tristan's sister, so it makes sense that she would go to him for something like that. She needed someone she could trust."

"Yeah, and I wasn't going to go there that night, Shon. I had no idea of who I was looking for, so I refused to sit in that place, scouting, and was gonna wait until Chench sent me the picture before I went back. He called me as soon as that guy got there and practically rushed me to get there. He was in on this shit, too. I never told you but he and Chaianne went out of town together that very next morning."

"I heard about that, too. Apparently, something went down between the two of them that same night. Mad people from Albany went to Atlantic City to watch that fight. I heard her new boyfriend saw them out and he and Chench almost got into it. I guess Vera's brother's best friend's cousin was there, and he said when he was leaving the after party, he saw Chench and the dread head dude in a standoff. Dread had a gun pointed at Chench and Chench was calling Chaianne stupid and dumb for being with a dude who was trying to kill her, or some crazy shit like that. But I heard no one really believed his story because he's a known liar and embellisher. However, Vera was still dealing with Chaianne's baby's father, off and on, and he practically confirmed that something did happen. He and their daughter had been in Jersey that weekend, seeing his family and she called him to pick her up from the hotel and bring her back to Albany."

Now, it was Whitney's turn to be stunned. She replayed her conversation with her father and, based on what Shon had just told her, the attempted hit on Chaianne must've been true. It was too much of a coincidence for it not to be. "Shit, Shon! What the hell did I do? I called Chench's phone, making threats and vowing to never speak to him again. Now, he probably thinks I'm a crazy lunatic and never wants to speak to *me* again." Whitney shook her head in disgust. "I've done some really mean shit lately and it all stems from my father telling me about his daughter. I wish I could undo all this mess. My life is ruined now." Whitney told Shon everything she plotted after finding out about Chaianne. From trying to take over her company and the double revenge plot by placing her and Mitch in one another's path. Whitney thought if she could get Mitch to do the crazy shit he was known to do, and scare Chaianne out of business, then that was one way of hurting her. And if that didn't work, then surely her MoneyWorx scheme would. Now, all she could think about was how it would have been easier to just give Chaianne a chance. The Mrs. Robinson plot was coming back to bite her in the ass, and she'd never be able to reconcile with Chench. Patrick had killed his father and he was now in prison, and she'd ended her relationship with her mother. It was all starting to weigh heavily on her.

"You know what, B to the FF, everyone makes mistakes. Some small, some big, some mean, but most fixable. You acted in poor judgment and thank God no one was seriously hurt behind it. You definitely went to the extreme to get back at Chaianne. That's what I mean about suburban chicks and hood chicks. I would've just beaten her ass ova and ova and ova and ova again, until she got tired and backed the fuck off. But you doing all this intricate plotting and shit…too much work for me. Like what made you think all that was even necessary?" Whitney shrugged pathetically. Shon empathized. "Listen, Bones, it's all good babe. Just continue to see your therapist and get the help you need to be the best version of yourself. I don't see you as all of your faults. I see a kind-hearted, smart, compassionate, brave, and hard-working woman. I see a beautiful black sista, who kicks ass and takes names later. I see a woman who is resilient and steadfast. You *will* get through this, my friend, and I will be right here with you every step of the way. As far as Chench, he'll come around. You had him wide open and he was feeling you just as much as you're feeling him. When it comes to Chaianne, I felt and still feel, like you should find it in you to embrace her. She might actually be a really cool person, as long as you aren't trying to sleep with her men." Shon laughed and Whitney did too. "If she's anything like you, I'm sure you are going to love her." Shon wrapped her arms around Whitney.

Whitney did the same to Shon and they held the hug for as long as they could before their backs started aching.

"Thank you! I really needed that. I can't tell you how much better I feel already." Whitney looked around the house. "I really appreciate you, Roshonda Garland. I don't think I could've gotten through this without you."

"I'm glad I could be here for you. You've been so good to me and my family that this is the least I could do." Shon wiped her friend's face. "I think we should go get pampered. I need a bikini wax, pedicure, a manicure, and some new lingerie." Shon smirked.

"Well, damn. What you trying to get into?"

"More like what's trying to get into me," Shon stated slyly.

"Yeah, right!" Whitney pursed her lips and turned away. She looked back at Shon. "Oh, my God! Is your man home?"

Shon giggled sheepishly and bit her lip. “Nope, not yet, but he will be next week! The parole officer called me yesterday and said everything was approved. My man is finally coming home, girl!”

Whitney screamed and squeezed her friend again. She was genuinely happy for Shon and the children. She was glad her friend’s family would be made whole again. Although she still had an aching feeling in her heart, she didn’t let that interfere with her happiness for Shon.

“This has been quite the year,” Shon said as she silently reflected on everything that had happened, the lows and the highs. She looked at Whitney with the side eye. “You know, what happened in Miami stays in Miami, right?”

“Oh, you mean never let what happened after that Roc-A-Fella concert slip out?” Whitney joked.

Shon swatted at her arm. “Bones!”

“Don’t worry, B to the FF, your secret is, and *always* will be, safe with me!”

Chapter Thirty-Eight

Months went by and seasons changed and Whitney still hadn't spoken to Chench. His phone was off and she didn't know where to find him. She rode by the bar intermittently, but never got out for fear of running into Tristan or someone else from that night. Having practically ended all sponsor-related activities, Whitney used that free time to help Shon plan and prepare for her quickly approaching wedding. That's why when she received a call from Dr. Blakemore, she was prepared to decline his request. To her surprise, he said he was happily married and about to welcome his first child. He had called for a mailing address as he wanted to give her the painting he had outbid her on. They had turned their home office that held the painting into a nursery and had no use for it. She happily accepted the gift and they met at a neutral location to make the exchange.

Unfortunately for MoneyWorx, after all that went down, Chaianne declined the offer and wanted to use the time to reevaluate everything. Whitney later found out from her dad, that after the attempt on Chaianne's life, she had taken a break while deciding where she wanted her business to go. In hindsight, Whitney couldn't blame her. After discovering all she had been through, because of Whitney's vengeance, it made sense.

Whitney decided to do the same thing. She took a leave of absence from the public defender's office and lived off her savings and residual income from her other business dealings. She had more than enough money saved to pay her bills for the next six months, without feeling strapped for cash.

Shon's wedding was upon them and she wanted nothing more than to have someone as fine as Chench on her arm for the occasion. She wasn't above begging and had reached out to him several times, but when she was told she had the wrong number, she gave up. Instead of sulking in her misery, she used the down time to work on herself as Shon had suggested. She's been maintaining consistent therapy, doing daily meditation, and even started a cycling class. She organized legitimate fundraisers to benefit the RJG Foundation and held clinics twice a month for members of the LBGTQ community in need of legal advice and guidance.

Whitney also gave up drugs and cut back her alcohol consumption to only social events. Her new skincare regimen was working wonders on her face, and she was looking more vibrant and refreshed than ever before. It wasn't just her who noticed the difference, either. Every single man and even some of the committed ones at Shon's wedding checked her out and respectfully complimented her at every turn. She hadn't experienced that kind of open attraction before and she couldn't deny that it felt damn good, especially from her own kind.

The longer she hung around Shon and Quavier, the more she interacted with black men of a different caliber. After Jason and Tristan, she had been almost certain she was done with that kind for good. Now, having been exposed to mature, classy, and respectful black men, she got to see a different side of her race.

After the wedding, Whitney congratulated the happy couple and blessed them with a gift she knew they'd enjoy once they made it to their honeymoon. She stopped at the gas station to get a bottle of water and some chewing gum before pumping her gas. When she walked out to her car, she was shocked to see Chench standing there, waiting for her.

"Now, you know I can't let you pump your own gas, right?" He smiled at her and proceeded to insert the pump into the gas tank. "I don't think I ever told you how good you look driving this cherry red Mercedes convertible. It suits you well, ma. I can't front, the 'TOPLESS' custom plates sealed the deal," he said.

Whitney barely listened to anything he said as she was still shocked that he was standing in front of her. "Where did you come from? Where have you been?" Whitney was happy to see him but curious as well.

"I had a lot going on, ma. I ain't gonna lie. That pregnancy shit fucked me up, too. We had a good thing going on. I was ready to give it all up for you, to make us work, but it was like I wasn't enough for you. Work, your lifestyle, traveling, all that shit came before me. That thing with Chai, it wasn't nuthin'. She had some wild shit goin' on and I was just tryin' to be a friend by taking her out of town. I can't front, she'll always have a piece of my heart, but we're done for good. She moved on."

Whitney appreciated his honesty but she needed reassurance. "What about you? Have you moved on? How long will she have your heart, Chench?"

He lowered his head for a moment and looked back up at Whitney. "Yeah, I'm ready to move on … with you. I can't deny, she might have a piece of me forever. That's just how I love, but that doesn't mean there isn't room for someone else."

"But that's not the way love goes. Someone doesn't just enter your life and make you stop loving the person you once shared your life with."

"That's true, and I agree to an extent. Chai made it clear that I'm not what she wants. She is moving on with her life and I'm doing the same. The only reason I kept her close and kept going back was because I hadn't found anything that made me feel secure enough to stay away. I needed you to want me like I wanted you, but that never happened."

"But I *do* want you, Chench. I've always wanted you. I just wasn't ready to give all of me to you at the time. For crying out loud, I didn't even know what love was until recently."

The gas pump clicked, signaling that the tank was full. He placed the pump back on the nozzle and tightened the gas cap. "So, are you saying that you know what love is now?"

Whitney walked up to him and placed her arms around his neck. She put her lips on his and kissed him slowly and passionately. They were locked in and unbothered by their surroundings.

"Wow," Chench commented. "I don't think I've ever been kissed like that before, especially not by you. So, does that mean I've finally penetrated that emotional muscle?" he asked.

Whitney smiled and bit her lip. "That's the way love goes, right?"

"Nah, fuck all that. I wanna hear you say it!"

"Say what?" Whitney poked.

"Don't play with me, girl."

"Alright, alright." She pulled her head away from his chest so she could look up into his eyes. "I love you, Chench, and I want to spend the rest of the day proving it."

They stood in each other's embrace until another driver waiting to use the gas pump honked at them. Whitney threw her hand up apologetically and told Chench to meet her at her home.

She was hoping Chench was right behind her but she had been home for over an hour before he arrived. She didn't have his new number, so she couldn't call him to see where he was or make sure he was okay. As soon as the thought entered her mind, the doorbell rang. When she opened it, Chench was on one knee with a bouquet of flowers and a small black velvet box.

"Whitney S. W. Bonesteel, will you marry me?"

A relationship can't be sustained if the foundation is built on lies. Her therapist's words quickly entered her mind. She hadn't even had the opportunity to reveal her truth to him.

"There's some things I haven't told you about me and if I do, you probably wouldn't ..."

Chench cut her off. "You said you love me. Was that true?"

"Yes, of course that was true."

"Well then that's all I need to know. So I'll ask again, will you marry me?"

Whitney thought back on all her dad's failed marriages, his infidelity, Chaianne's hold on Chench, her ability to move on in spite of their failed relationship. She thought of Shon and how happy she seemed. She also thought of Jackson and how empty his passing had left her. Whitney thought of the life she had been living and realized it was lonely. If Chench was willing to ask for her hand in marriage despite her flaws and their history, then she had nothing to lose.

"Yes, yes, Chench. I will marry you!"

He placed the ring on her finger and lifted her up off her feet. Once he got her inside, he closed the door with his foot and led her straight to their favorite room in the house.

Discussion Questions

- Was Whitney too hard on her parents? Specifically her mom?
- Was she wrong for not giving Chaianne a fair chance?
- Should Whitney have been more understanding of Patrick's desire for her?
- Why couldn't Whitney get from Lina and Simone what she got from Jackson and Shon?
- Do you think she should give black men a chance?
- Were her reasons for not dating men of her race justified?
- Besides not wanting children, why else do you think she didn't keep Chench's baby?
- What do you think was the number one reason Whitney didn't embrace Chaianne?
- Do you think Whitney and Chench will last?

Thank you so much for reading my work! If you enjoyed this book please leave a review and recommend it to others. Feel free to connect with me via email at VyAntenette@gmail.com

Made in the USA
Middletown, DE
23 February 2020

84971434R00159